THE JOURNEY HOME

A 1932 SIDEQUEL

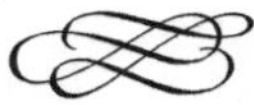

KAREN M COX

PRAISE FOR KAREN M COX

1932

"...a truly fresh take on this timeless tale." *Bustle.com*

Bronze Medal for Romance: Independent Publisher Book Awards, 2011

FIND WONDER IN ALL THINGS

"...stands on its own and no wonder at all, why it was awarded the Gold Medal in the Romance category at the 2012 Independent Publisher Book Awards." *Austenprose*

Finalist: 2013 Next Generation Indie Book Awards in Romance category

UNDECEIVED

Best of 2016 lists: *Margie's Must Reads, Babblings of a Bookworm, Just Jane 1813*

"...an incredibly unique and riveting tale..." *Austenesque Reviews*

I COULD WRITE A BOOK

"Perceptive and compelling" *Austenesque Reviews*

"a great reimagining of *Emma,* in a fabulous setting" *Olga Author Translator*

SON OF A PREACHER MAN
"...a beautiful, impressive story." *With Love For Books*
"...a heartwarming story that had a strong flavor of nostalgia that was tempered with bittersweet reality." *Night Owl Book Cafe*

PROLOGUE

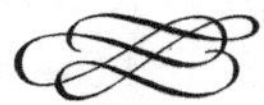

APRIL 21, 1931

*M*y heart jumped in response to the sharp slam of the front door. I sank down onto the couch, hands covering my face as uncontrolled sobs shook my shoulders. My cheek still stung where he struck me, and I knew there would be a bruise to hide tomorrow. The pressure of my child's hand on my knee drew me out of my grief, and I peered down at the little one beside me. Her dark eyes seemed to take up half her gaunt face. I pulled her into my embrace and hugged her tightly.

"I'm sorry, my darling. Mama's so, so very sorry." I pulled back to take a careful look at my daughter. Tears coursed down her little face, but no sound came from her mouth.

"Are you hurt? Tell Mama what hurts."

Her tiny mouth set into a grim line. She shook her head in determination and refused to utter a word. Suddenly, I heard the weak sound of a newborn's cry from the other room. My baby would need to be fed again soon. I had no idea how there could be any milk left in

1

my body at all. I had eaten nothing but cornbread and a little milk in the last four days.

"I need to get the baby, sweetheart. I'll be right back."

My little Maggie grabbed onto my skirt, walking with me as I went to retrieve tiny Ruth Anne—Maggie refusing to leave the safety of my presence. The three of us sat on the couch as the sun began to set: baby at my breast, toddler attached firmly to my side. We remained long after the baby had finished nursing and Maggie had drifted off to sleep. I was lost in my thoughts, and the tears returned.

The time had come. I had to get away. My heart was breaking in a thousand pieces, but I had to pick up what was left of my life. My children deserved better than this, and I would do anything to make sure they had it. Gently, I laid the baby in the bassinet and my older daughter on the bed, covering her with a threadbare blanket.

Exhausted, but driven by an adrenaline born of fear and purpose, I dragged an old worn-out trunk from the closet. It had seen more use in the last year than in the previous twenty years, I was certain. I dashed around the hovel of an apartment where we lived, collecting the barest necessities, but then, I stopped. *Where can I go?* I was weak from giving birth—weak from hunger and living in poverty. I had no job and no money. At least here, there was shelter. There was a little bit of food.

I always believed that marriage was forever, and that my place was with my husband. My face crumpled in a fresh round of grief, as I remembered this latest insult to my pride, to my heart. I knew my husband wasn't the man I fell in love with, but this? I never expected this. At first, I didn't believe the policemen who came searching for him. When my husband finally came back and I confronted him, though, he confirmed the awful truth. For the last four years, I had been living a lie. My married name wasn't my name at all. My husband had another life, another wife and other children who lived far away. When he disappeared for weeks at a time, did he go home to them? Did that woman know about his other family? Did he love her? Or did he despise her the way he had come to despise the wife and daughters holed up in this broken-down apartment building? Did he have other little girls? Or a son?

Another sob escaped me as I realized what this meant for my girls. I was an unmarried woman with two children that were…illegitimate. That was the kind word. The ugly word suddenly roared into my mind; people would say my precious babies were bastards.

His betrayal was complete, my situation hopeless. I sobbed until my breath was ragged.

Out of the blue, an almost forgotten alternative occurred to me. Would my brother possibly let me come back home? I had never returned because I didn't want to disgrace my family. I had shamed myself by running away. How could I bear my brother's stern, forbidding face? I had been such a burden to him all those years since our parents died. And yet…

I looked at the sleeping children in the bedroom. I went over and brushed a dark curl off Maggie's face, and my heart broke anew with a mother's all-encompassing love. My emotions darted this way and that, from anxiety to anger to grief, to terror and uncertainty. Eventually, those scattered thoughts and feelings ran headfirst into the foundation of my soul, given to me by my Maker and made of the strongest steel. That part of me could not be bruised, could not be broken by mere words and blows, or by my own self-doubt. Now, the foundation was glowing red with a steady, warming heat, and I could hear a voice speaking words that were still faint and unformed.

I closed my eyes tightly and prayed. *Please God, just tell me what to do and I will do it, no matter what the cost to me. Help me and help my children. What should I do? Where should I go?*

"*Hush,*" the voice whispered. "*Be still and listen.*" I calmed and took a deep breath, my eyes still closed. The answer formed in my mind, at first without words and then without sound but clearly discernible nonetheless. It said…

"*Go home.*"

CHAPTER 1

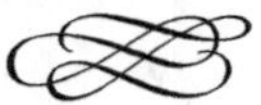

JUNE 3, 1931

"Georgiana, the sheriff is here." My brother, William, stood in the parlor doorway, his somber expression gauging my reaction to our visitor's arrival.

I had spread out a blanket to play peek-a-boo with the baby, but my gaze darted upwards from my seat on the floor. I was momentarily paralyzed. Dread welled up inside me, making my pulse race and my palms sweat. Every visitor, every acquaintance I encountered since my return home triggered this reaction. Maggie, my three-year-old, played beside me, content yet silent, holding the birthday gift her Uncle William brought her from Nashville last week. She had spent the last ten minutes repeatedly putting the doll to bed—complete with covers and good night kisses—and waking it up. Now, she eased closer to me, watched my expression as if trying to ascertain whether she should be on her guard.

Despite my good intentions—I wanted to be brave for my girls—my eyes filled with unshed tears. "Oh William, I don't want to see anyone."

He came in and sat down beside me. "Gigi." The childhood nick-name rolled gently off his tongue, reminding me of all the times he comforted me when I was a child and had a nightmare or thought there might be a monster under my bed. "You've been to church a few times now, gone shopping in Meryton, and each time it's been all right. Don't you see that no one around here is going to snub you or speak unkindly to you?"

"Perhaps not to my face," I answered in a soft, small voice. "Besides, no one at church knows what happened, at least, not for sure. You still want me to tell the sheriff the whole story, don't you?"

William frowned. "I thought we agreed. If we're asking for his help, he needs to know exactly where you've been, what you've been through."

I looked away to avoid the pity I knew I would see in his expression. "I know. It's just...how can I look him in the eye? I'm so ashamed. I was so stupid."

He turned my chin and brought my face around to look at him. "Georgiana," he said solemnly, "you were *not* stupid. You were young and naïve, and a wicked man took advantage of you. I wish to God that I had been there to protect you, but I wasn't. It still grieves me. Sheriff Fitzwilliam knows all of that."

My lip trembled, and I swallowed the urge to cry again.

William went on in a gentle voice. "I'm not trying to make you feel ashamed. I just want you to see that Richard can be trusted. He's been a good friend to me, and he's seen many situations like yours over the years. Give him the benefit of the doubt. He has a soft heart for women and children."

I nodded and looked back at the ground. Maggie wiggled into my lap, looking up at her uncle with dark, defiant eyes. She pushed against his shoulder.

"Sorry, Maggie." He gave her a quiet smile. My daughter silently protested like this whenever he touched me, even if it was only to take my elbow or pat me on the back.

He shook his head. "I wish she'd quit staring at me like that. It's unnerving."

I laughed through my tears, softly, so as not to frighten the toddler in my lap. "I don't know why it bothers you. She looks just like you do half the time." Maggie's dark-eyed stare was the little-girl version of William's curmudgeonly scowl.

"I do not stare like that," he insisted.

I gave the little girl in my arms a quick squeeze, and my shaky sigh escaped into the room. "Go ahead and bring the sheriff in here. I might as well get this over with."

William's gentle smile gave me a tiny boost of strength. "That's my girl." He stood up and exited the room.

A few minutes later, I heard the low rumble of men's voices outside and hurried to stand just behind the curtain that covered the screen window. I could see the murky shadow of William's form as he escorted the sheriff up the front steps and across the porch. Maggie looked up at me, her dark eyes as big as saucers.

"It's all right, darling," I said to reassure myself as much as her. "Sheriff and Uncle are nice men." The footsteps halted right outside the front door. They lowered their voices, but I heard the conversation anyway.

"She's agreed to speak with you now. I had to talk her into it. She's still very fragile, Richard."

"I'll only ask what I need to, and whenever I can, I'll ask you instead of her."

"I think that's probably wise. "

"Um…William?" The sheriff began awkwardly.

"Yes?"

"I'm not sure how to say this, so I'll just come right out with it."

William paused, and my mind whirled in an anxious dance with my heartbeat. "Yes?" he repeated slowly.

The sheriff cleared his throat and continued in a forced business-like tone. "I know you're taking care of things on the legal end with the marriage and the birth certificates. And I'm helping with the enforcement end. I'll do whatever I can to keep him away from her." My heart surged upwards, buoyed by the confident tone of his voice. "But what about her health?"

"Her health?"

"Has she seen a doctor since she came back? Have the girls?"

William sounded relieved, and his voice grew louder. "Oh. Yes, I took them to the doctors at Vanderbilt, soon after they arrived. The doctor says Georgiana's healing well after the birth, and the rest of the issues, like the anemia, will be resolved with good food and rest. Well, except for Maggie not talking. But the doctor says she'll talk again when she feels safe, so…"

"William"—Sheriff Fitzwilliam lowered his voice to an urgent whisper, so soft I could barely hear him—"what I mean is, given the bigamy charge, it is unlikely that the scoundrel was faithful to her. Did you make sure the doctor checked her for what they call the bad blood disease, for syphilis?"

Now I found myself suffocating under a blanket of abject mortification.

"Good Lord, Richard!" My brother's face turned five different shades of red. "Why would you ask me such a thing?"

"Because there's a new medicine called Salversan, and it has a better chance of working early on, that's why." There was another awkward moment. I could almost feel the disgrace lingering on my skin. I knew the sheriff was right; I even thought the same thing myself, after I realized where my husband might have been, but it sounded so embarrassing when someone else mentioned it.

"I'm sorry, but I wasn't sure if you knew to ask, and it's important. She might not even realize anything was wrong or get the treatment until it was too late. I don't want to offend you, but I've seen way too much, doing this job."

William sighed. "Don't apologize. You were right. I didn't think to ask the doctor about that." He paused. "But she did." I closed my eyes in despairing disbelief. How could William tell a virtual stranger such a private thing about me? My humiliation was now complete.

I could hear the surprise in Richard's voice. "Oh?"

"She's safe from that burden at least. She's had to discover evils no woman should ever have to learn, and it torments me."

Richard clapped him on the shoulder as they entered the house, and the sound of their footsteps reverberated in the hallway. "She's home, and everything's going to be all right now."

I picked up the baby and cradled her in the crook of my arm. Somehow, I swallowed my embarrassment and kept the tears at bay. Maggie clung to the hem of my skirt, shooting wary looks at the door. Finally, William entered, followed by Richard Fitzwilliam.

I barely remembered him from years ago, when I lived at home before boarding school. I vaguely recalled a young man with a pleasant smile and a pretty wife. I don't know what I was expecting when he came through that door and I got a good look at him, but the man standing before me wasn't it. For one thing, he was not a towering, swaggering fellow like I imagined a sheriff might be. He wasn't too much taller than me, and his eyes held a gentle, blue warmth that warmed my insides. Remembering the conversation I had just overheard, I reflexively dropped my gaze until William called my name.

"Georgiana, you remember Sheriff Fitzwilliam, don't you? He has some good news for us."

"Miss Darcy, it's good to see you again." He smiled at me and turned his attention to the baby in my arms.

"This your little one?" he asked, reaching his finger out to let her grasp it in her chubby little hand.

"Yes sir," I replied. "This is Ruth."

Sheriff Fitzwilliam looked down suddenly, and his face broke into a surprised smile. My dark headed toddler had both hands on his knee, pushing him away from us.

"Maggie! Stop, darling. It's all right." I reached down and clasped my daughter's hand, gently drawing her back. "I'm sorry, Sheriff. She's a little shy." *Like me,* I wanted to explain.

William gave his friend a meaningful look. "She doesn't like anyone except Mrs. Reynolds to touch them." A mirthless chuckle escaped his mouth. "Not even me."

Richard looked at me with kindness but not with pity. He addressed me, rather than my brother, and I could see how William would be able to tell him private information without a second thought. His expression was open and accepting, without a hint of disapproval.

"Understandable," he said softly.

Slowly, he squatted down until he was eye-level with Maggie. She backed up and grabbed my skirt hem, giving him a piercing glare.

"Hello, sugar bean. It's good to meet you too." He smiled, but he didn't approach or touch her, showing that he had good intuition about frightened children. So many times, people tried to force her to speak to them, but he just let her look her fill at him and then, he stood back up.

"Shall we?" William indicated the chairs in the parlor.

I settled the children back on the blanket and took a chair near my brother and his friend. I sat, perched on the edge of my seat, wringing my hands in my lap. The next half-hour was spent in excruciating exposition, detailing the last four years of my life. Sheriff Fitzwilliam asked some questions, most of which were answered by William, and he took a few notes. He folded the cover over his pad of paper and gave me a friendly smile.

"Well, as William said when we came in, I do have good news for you, ma'am. The fiend is definitely out of the state now, and I don't think he'll be bothering you anymore. The feds are lookin' for him, and every police department from Nashville to Bowling Green knows to keep an eye out and let me know if he comes around these parts. I made sure of that."

I heaved a sigh of relief. "Thank you, Sheriff."

"No thanks necessary. I'm glad to do it. I only wish I could tell you he's in custody, but we'll hold out hope for that, won't we?"

I nodded, taking stock of the features of his face: strong jaw, sandy hair, blue-as-the-summer-sky eyes that were already adorned with a few crows' feet at the corners. His nose was a bit crooked about halfway down, indicating it had been broken once long ago. All in all, a handsome face.

William spoke up, breaking into my thoughts. "Richard has put me in touch with the vital statistics departments in Indiana and Illinois.

My attorney has drawn up the papers to change the girls' last name to Darcy, if that's still what you want."

I looked him in the eye, and my voice took on a hard quality I didn't recognize. "I don't want my daughters to have any part of that man. As far as they are concerned, he never existed." On this point, my mind was made up.

The sheriff's eyes widened a little. "The young'uns may ask you someday."

"Hopefully, it will be a long while before they do. And perhaps, by then, I'll have come up with something to tell them."

"We'll do whatever you wish, Georgiana." William's voice held a note of sadness that nearly broke my heart.

"Thank you."

"Well, then…" The sheriff put on his hat and stood. "I'll be off. You'll call me if you need anything else?"

William extended his hand. "We're much obliged to you, Richard."

"As I said, I'm glad to do whatever I can." He looked over at me. "Miss Darcy…"

"Yes?"

He gazed at me for what seemed like a long time, but then he straightened up, shooting a surreptitious look at my brother. "Welcome home."

CHAPTER 2

DECEMBER 24, 1931

The front door slammed, and a cold blast of winter wind entered the parlor, making the flames in the fireplace dip and swirl. I heard a softly growled "Damnation!" from the foyer, and a grin spread unbidden across my face. Maggie turned from her tea set in the corner of the room and ran to the door. She whirled back around to look at me, her eyes wild with excitement.

"Uncle's back with the Christmas tree, little darling."

She nodded enthusiastically and scooted back from the doorway when an eight-foot evergreen walked into the room. A dark head poked out from behind it.

"It took me two hours to find this thing and drag it back here," he grumbled.

"I told you that you could have bought one in town. Mr. Jennings is selling them."

"Hmmph. This one's better."

I smiled to myself. He was enjoying the Christmas spirit more than he wanted to admit, the old Scrooge!

"Did you find the lights?" he asked.

"Yes, they came in last week. Mrs. Reynolds stored them in the back room. I found the ornaments, too—up in the attic. Didn't you use them last year?"

"No."

"What did you decorate the tree with?"

William leaned the evergreen against the wall and assembled the tree stand. "Didn't have a tree." He grunted as he lifted the tree and inserted it in the stand.

"Oh."

"Is this straight?" he asked.

I tilted my head and looked at the tree thoughtfully. "A little to the right I think."

He disappeared under the lowest boughs again and made a few adjustments.

"There, that's better."

The sound of a baby crying disturbed the bustling quiet of unwrapping ornaments and William fiddling with the tree.

Maggie came over and tugged on my sleeve. "Yes, darling, I hear her. I'm on my way up there."

"Where's Mrs. Reynolds?" William asked, looking around for our gray-haired but still spry housekeeper.

"She went to visit her sister in Franklin for Christmas. She'll be back this evening."

"You stay there and finish unpacking the ornaments. I'll get the baby," he volunteered.

"She'll probably need a diaper change." I thought he deserved a warning.

"I can do that."

"Don't poke her with a pin."

"I have changed her before."

William disappeared and returned in a few minutes with my blue-eyed cherub in his arms. Her white hair swirled around her head like a halo, and she was rubbing her eyes to wipe the sleep out of them. She gave me a shy smile and tucked her head against her uncle's shoulder. He kissed her hair.

William sat down on the sofa and cuddled her in his arms so she could see the room, nestling her head beneath his chin. "William, you're so good with children. You'd make a wonderful father."

He smiled at me in acknowledgement but didn't respond.

"You should marry and have a family of your own."

He shrugged his shoulders.

"Why haven't you?" I asked, genuinely curious.

"I did try once."

I winced. *How could I not remember about Anne?* "I'm sorry. I didn't think. It was just so long ago, and I…"

William's voice was low and reassuring. "It's all right."

We sat in silence while I unpacked more ornaments.

"Oooh, look!" I held up a sparkly angel, dressed in ivory moire taffeta with spun gold hair and translucent wings. "I remember this one!"

He gave me a quizzical smile.

"Mother's Aunt Sophie sent this one Christmas. Goodness, I couldn't have been any more than six years old. Don't you remember?"

"I'm afraid I don't. I haven't looked through those in some time."

I brought the angel down to my lap and looked at my brother. "When was the last time you did put up a tree?"

"Probably the last year you were home. No reason to go through all this trouble just for me."

My expression must have shown my sympathy, because he frowned at me.

"What? Don't look at me that way. It wasn't that much of a deprivation. Mrs. Reynolds went to see her sister on Christmas Day every year, and I went to Bowling Green and spent Christmas with Aunt Catherine."

"And for that alone, I'm sorry I left," was my sarcastic reply.

William's lips quirked into a sardonic smile. "She's not that bad."

"I'm glad you think so. I invited her for Christmas dinner tomorrow." *And* that *certainly took some courage!*

He raised an eyebrow.

"Even though Mrs. Reynolds threatened to stay in Franklin with her sister if I did."

"Gi—"

"Oh, Mrs. Reynolds was teasing, of course."

"You didn't have to—"

I shrugged. "Catherine's our family, and she's all alone except for that butler of hers. Poor Louis. He worships the ground she walks on, and she treats him like dirt."

"She will probably say something to you about your…situation."

"Yes, I know. But I'm so glad to be home, I think I can even take that."

"I won't let her insult you in your own house."

"I'll give her a wide berth. She won't be too harsh if you're around anyway."

Maggie had been sitting beside me, helping unpack ornaments—holding them up for me to see and waiting for the "oohs" and "aahhs" I voiced for her. She got up now and walked over to stand in front of William. She watched him sit with Ruth in his arms, playing Pat-A-Cake for a few minutes, staring at him until he noticed her.

"Hello there, Maggie Moo." It was a precious little nickname he'd given her one morning while we were walking around the farm, trying in vain to get her to say something—anything. She'd made so much progress since we'd returned to Pemberley. How I wished she would make a full recovery and resume talking!

He extended a hand to her. She stared at it, and then back at him, unmoving.

"If I'm so good with children, how come I can't get this one to even talk to me?"

His comment distressed me, but I tried to keep my voice light and hopeful. I parroted the children's doctor we saw in Nashville. "She'll come around eventually."

William got up and leaned over to hand Ruth to me. Then, he pulled out his pocket knife and opened the brand-new box of lights.

"How about we get these lights on the tree?" he asked Maggie. He had taken the doctor's advice to heart and talked to her about every-thing they did together, never once demanding a response that she was either unable or unwilling to give.

She approached him, watching as he drew out the string of bulbs.

"Let's hope they all work. If one goes, they all go," he muttered under his breath. He plugged in the string and glowing spheres of red, green, yellow and blue appeared, casting warm colored light on the floor and walls around them.

Maggie gasped.

William and I both looked at her to make sure she wasn't frightened, but all we saw was a rapt expression of wonder on her face.

"Now, I'll unplug them and put them on the tree," he explained. She looked up at him and nodded.

He walked around, arranging lights on cedar-scented branches. I handed Maggie the ornaments one by one, and she carried them to her uncle. He continued talking with her, putting them on the tree under the direction of her pointing finger. Sometimes I gave my two-cents worth on where they should go—more expensive or sentimen-tally valuable ones were placed out of the reach of little hands, for example. But mostly, I let them decorate together while I played with Ruth.

We were sitting in the parlor after dinner, admiring the tree and listening to the radio, when William got up and walked into his study. He returned with a few wrapped packages and began handing them out.

"William, what is this? Christmas isn't until tomorrow."

"I didn't want Saint Nick to steal my glory. We're opening these tonight."

I laughed as I took a small square box from his hand; he never could keep presents a secret for very long. "Thank you."

He placed a soft, oddly wrapped present next to Ruth, who was sitting on the floor beside me. Next, he went to Maggie and set two packages in front of her. He had learned she rarely took anything directly from his hand.

I helped Ruth open her teddy bear and glanced over at my older daughter, who was tentatively tearing the paper on her package.

"Open yours," he urged me.

I ripped the paper off the box with enthusiasm, revealing a red, cloth-covered container underneath. I opened the hinged lid and gingerly touched the necklace resting inside.

"Oh! It's beautiful." I lifted the silver chain out of the box and held it up to the light. The charm was a silver cross, entwined with flowers and leaves. "Thank you!" He looked so pleased at my gratitude, it made my heart melt. I couldn't imagine how lonely he must have been while I was gone.

"Merry Christmas, Gi." He cleared his throat and looked over at Maggie. She was holding the wooden box in her hand, looking at it and then at him. He said nothing, but reached out his hand, palm up. She put the box in his grasp, and he turned it over.

"See, little one? It's a music box. You wind it here…" He turned the little key on the bottom. "Now, you open the lid, and it plays music." He held it out to her. "Go ahead—you open it."

She lifted the lid, and a little ballerina stood up in the middle of the box. The tinkling sound of the "Dance of the Sugar Plum Fairy" erupted from under the ballerina's feet. Maggie looked at it in wonder and took it from his hand, examining the box, opening and closing the lid and looking underneath it.

"Open this present too." He gestured toward the flat package sitting beside her.

"William," I admonished. "You shouldn't spoil her so." His indulgence was endearing, but it could easily get out of hand, if I let it.

"This one is for all of us," he said defensively. What could I say? He always had a reason for his gifts, which made it particularly difficult to dissuade him.

He helped Maggie tear the paper and carefully remove the present inside.

"Remember this, Gigi?" He turned the book so I could see the cover.

A flash of recognition bolted through me. *'Twas the Night Before Christmas.* Is that the one—?"

"Yep," he beamed. "That's the one Father brought us from Nashville that winter. You remember? It snowed so hard, we weren't sure he would make it back in time for Christmas Eve dinner."

"Yes! And after dinner, he read it to us before we went to sleep." I sighed. "That was a lovely Christmas."

"It was." William spent a few minutes lost in his memories, a ghost of a smile on his face. Then, he picked up the *Courier-Journal* sitting on the end table. Maggie sat cross-legged on the floor, looking at the pictures in the book while she gently turned the pages. Ruth was pounding her teddy bear's head against the floor and trying to eat his paws. William opened the paper to read, looking every few minutes over the top of it at our idyllic little scene. His expression shone with contentment, the best Christmas present I'd ever received from him.

That was when Maggie got up and walked over to me. Unbelievably, she whispered a question in my ear. She hadn't spoken any words except for an infrequently whispered "Mama" for eight long months!

"I don't know, darling. Why don't you ask him?" I replied, a frisson of excitement in my voice.

William looked down at the pat on his knee. He looked incredulous; Maggie was holding the book out to him. "What is it, Maggie Moo?" he asked, out of habit.

"Read it, Unca." Her little voice cut through the room like the peal of a church bell. William's eyes opened wide in shock, but he took the book from her with slightly shaking hands. He looked up at me. I clasped my hand to my mouth to prevent a sob of joy from escaping; my eyes were filled with happy tears.

He cleared his throat. "Read it, you say?"

Maggie nodded.

"Well, you better hop up here, so you can see the pictures."

She climbed up on the sofa and lifted his elbow to settle herself on his lap in the crook of his arm. She looked over at me. "Mama." She patted the sofa beside them. "Bring baby here." She met her uncle's dark eyes with her own. "Read it now."

I scrambled up and practically dragged Ruth over to the sofa, barely able to contain my excitement. The baby struggled slightly, oblivious to the electric emotions permeating the room.

William cleared his throat again, opened the book and began.

"'Twas the Night before Christmas and all through the house,

Not a creature was stirring, not even a mouse."

Maggie giggled. William looked over her head at me; his dimpled smile lit up the room.

After he finished the book, Maggie took it from him and wriggled down to sit on the floor at his feet and looked through the pictures again.

I stared at my brother in tearful awe. "It's a miracle, a real Christmas miracle. I don't know how to thank you."

He shook his head, bewildered. "I wish I could take credit for it, Gi. But somehow, I don't think I'm responsible. It's God's work, not mine."

I nodded, unable to speak more. We watched my little girl look through the pictures two or three times before gathering our wits enough to announce that it was time to go to bed. After all, we all wanted Saint Nicholas to visit for real, didn't we?

It was God's work, I knew that, but my brother was God's instrument that day. I knew I would never forget that Christmas Eve— the night my baby decided to come back to us.

CHAPTER 3

MAY 18, 1932

I sat on the ground, bent over the strawberry plants arranged neatly in rows and picked up one of the vines. A breeze lifted the brim of my hat and cooled my brow. I closed my eyes and tilted my face to the warm spring sun. A bird's warble grew louder as it approached and then faded away as it flew off into the distance. An involuntary smile crossed my lips as I listened to my daughters' one-sided conversation.

"No, Ruth! Don't pick that one. Unca says you only pick the ones that's red all over. They're the only ones that's ripe. That one still gots white on it." I heard a tussle of movement, but still kept my eyes closed, listening to the spring morning all around me.

"Let go of it!"

"Aaaahhh!" Ruth's frustrated screech blared out into the humid morning air.

I opened my eyes and called to them. "Girls…"

Maggie strode over to me, pursing her lips in a grim line before setting her basket on the ground. Arms akimbo, she began in a haughty voice. "Mama! Ruth picks all the berries, even white and green ones! And she puts leaves in there! Look!" Maggie pointed at her collection of berries and sighed dramatically.

"It's fine, darling. We'll fish them out later."

"But Unca said only red ones taste good!"

"Uncle's right, but Ruth doesn't understand that yet—"

"But Unca said—"

"Margaret"—I spoke sharply—"that's enough. We'll sort through them when we get back to the house. It won't take that long. Ruth can't have picked that many white and green ones."

Maggie scowled with fury and turned to stomp away, but halted when a tall form cast a shadow over her. She stepped back and reached instinctively for me, and I shielded my eyes to look up.

"Oh hello, Sheriff."

"Ma'am." He tipped his hat. "Mornin', Miss Maggie." He tipped his hat to her as well. "Miss Ruth givin' you fits with your berries?"

Maggie sniffed. "No, sir."

"Ah," he replied, smiling. "So, you like them bitter white ones, do ya?"

"No, sir."

"No. And I don't blame you either. Let's see if we can talk some sense into her."

Maggie stared at him with big eyes, her brow furrowed in a little scowl.

"If you don't look just like Darcy in his worst mood, I'm a monkey's uncle," he muttered, then looked up sharply as my surprised laugh pealed through the air. I hadn't meant to laugh, but his observations mirrored mine exactly, and I couldn't help it.

"She does look like William. I think so too."

Richard was sporting an embarrassed smile that was nothing short of adorable. "I meant no offense ma'am. I didn't mean for you to hear me."

I waved my hand in a dismissive gesture. "None taken. Neither one of the girls looks much like me, although Ruth resembles me a little more. Maggie looks more like her..." I froze in mid-sentence. My gaze darted up to the sheriff, who was looking down at me with a surprised expression.

"Uncle William," he finished.

I stood up, looking down, around, anywhere but at the piercing blue gaze I felt all over my skin. "Of course." How could I have been so careless? Maggie was old enough to ask questions now; I needed to be more vigilant about my words, unless I wanted to explain some painful truths. Today, though, I didn't wince or cower under the ugly specter of the man who had been my husband. I guess the old adage was right; time had healed me, at least, in part. Then again, it had always been easier to face my past in Richard's—I mean, the sheriff's —presence.

He turned and knelt beside Ruth, who was squatting on the ground, picking every berry on the vine and making a neat pile on the red Kentucky earth beside her. Her face was smeared with dirt, and her white blond curls were blowing in the wind.

"Hey, cutie pie, look here." He picked a red berry and took a bite of it. "Mmm." He held it out to her and she took a bite too, red juice dripping down her chin.

"Mmm," she mimicked.

"Now," he picked a white one and tasted it, making a face and spitting it out. "Shoo!" He held it out to her and she took a bite, letting her tongue hang from her mouth as the berry fell out and hit the ground, along with a string of drool. I giggled.

He chuckled too, but shook his head and said, "Don't pick those. Shoo, yuck!"

"Yuck!"

"Here Maggie, come show her again. She might understand now. But don't get too cross if she still makes a mistake or two."

The sheriff stood up and caught me smiling at him. *Soft heart for children, indeed.* His easy-going grin spread across his face, and my heart sped up.

"So, what brings you out here, Sheriff?" I stepped close to him and lowered my voice. "You don't have bad news for me, do you?"

He shook his head. "Oh no. No, ma'am." He seemed a little discombobulated, so I backed up a step, thinking I'd made him uncomfortable.

"Uhh… just came by to see your brother actually."

"He's gone over to Bowling Green for the afternoon. Buying some equipment at an auction, I think. So, I'm afraid you've missed him."

"Ah." Richard stood there, fiddling with the hat in his hands. "You want some help with those?" He indicated the basket on the ground near my feet.

"If you like."

He put his hat back on and grabbed an empty basket as he headed to the row behind the girls. He leaned toward me and lowered his voice as he passed. "I didn't mean to bring up a touchy subject before."

"It's no matter."

"I'm sure it's been difficult for you, since you come back."

I sank back down on my knees and began putting berries in my basket again. What could I say? I didn't want him to think me one of those pitiful, defeated creatures. I wanted him to think I was strong. For some reason, gaining his respect was very important to me. I tried on a practical, business-like voice. "Not nearly as difficult as it was *before* I came back. Now, my children are clothed and fed, my daughter is talking again, and I don't live in constant fear of what tomorrow brings."

Sheriff Fitzwilliam sat up on his heels, watching me carefully. "At least you don't seem bitter."

I looked to the next plant, smiling, although I certainly didn't feel like it. "Then you're not looking very closely. Sometimes I am extremely bitter. But then, some days are more difficult than others."

"I understand how that goes."

"Do you?" How could he understand the burden of guilt I carried? I didn't want to be molly-coddled and gave him a skeptical look.

His blue eyes reached back across time. Then he brought his gaze back to me. "Yes," he replied softly, "I do understand."

Slowly, I processed his last words and quickly looked down, embarrassed. "Of course you do. You've had a loss as well. It didn't occur to me."

"It's no matter." He reflected my earlier words back to me. "It was long ago."

We continued working in silence for several minutes. I watched as his calloused hands quickly and efficiently stripped the vines of ripe berries, wondering at this gift he had for bringing out the strength hidden inside me.

"Sheriff?"

"Yes?"

"I appreciate your concern, but you don't need to comfort me about my sorrows. I guess we both know what it's like to have a broken heart. I really have no choice but to go on with my life, like you did all those years ago. So, let's not dwell on the past now." I held my breath, waiting for his answer.

He squinted up at me and then smiled broadly, holding out his berry-stained hand. "You've got yourself a deal there, Miss Darcy."

After shaking his hand, I stood up and brushed the dust from my skirt. "I think we've got enough of these berries."

"What are you doing with them anyway?"

A little voice piped up from the next row over. "We're making strawberry ice cream." Maggie came to stand beside us.

I placed a gentle hand on my daughter's head, smoothing a lock of her hair behind her ear.

"Do you like ice cream?" Maggie asked. "You can have some. We'll have lots to share."

"That's very kind of you, darling, but perhaps the sheriff has somewhere else to go."

"Well…" Richard paused, considering the offer. Then he shrugged. "Don't mind if I do. I got no place to be, and strawberry ice cream sounds mighty fine to me. I'll even turn the crank a time or two, to earn my share." He winked at Maggie.

Ruth reached for me, and I swung her up, sticky hands and all. Maggie picked up her little basket and put a basket in my other hand.

We turned and headed for the house. Richard sidled up beside me and took the basket, giving me another handsome smile. I returned a brief smile of my own and looked back at the ground. The blue warmth in his eyes was beginning to melt my heart, and that was a complication I certainly didn't need. Not now.

CHAPTER 4

AUGUST 2, 1932

"*S*ir, excuse me. Could you please tell me what time the train from Springfield arrives?" I was out of breath from running by the time I reached the ticket window.

"Springfield? No train come from Springfield today, miss." The ticket master spoke thickly around the wad of chewing tobacco in his cheek. I swallowed my disgust and tried not to make a face.

"Not Springfield, Kentucky, sir, Springfield, Illinois." I felt a tug on my skirt.

"Oh, Illinois. Well, let's see here." He spat into a container thankfully hidden behind the counter and got out a paper schedule. "You see, the train wouldn't come straight from Springfield, honey. It probably come from Louisville or Cincinnati."

"Yes, yes, I know." My impatience with this man was growing by the second. "What time does it arrive? I'm supposed to pick up my brother, and I'm afraid I've missed the train."

"Mama." Maggie tugged my skirt again.

"Just a minute, darling."

"Well, that's the thing." He squinted at me, yellow teeth flashing as he talked. "Springfield wouldn't be on my paper here. You don't know which way he come?"

"No, I'm afraid I don't. I—"

"Mama," Maggie repeated a little louder.

I closed my eyes in frustration. "I'm trying to find out what time Uncle's train gets here."

"This is 'portant."

"What is it, Margaret? I'm losing my patience." I turned to look sternly at her.

"Ruth ran that way." She pointed into the crowd behind us.

I gasped, and my eyes immediately began to search for white blond curls. "Ruth!" I left the man at the window and dodged and ducked among the crowd at the station, calling frantically for my younger daughter. I was practically dragging Maggie behind me, although she was trying her best to keep up.

"Oh, dear Lord! Where is she? Ruth!"

"I'm sorry Mama." Maggie's lip quivered. "She pulled me, and I couldn't hold on."

"It's not your fault, darling, but we have to find her right now!" I forced myself not to think about the dangers train stations posed to toddlers.

"Ruth!" Maggie's little voice rang above the crowd.

I broke through another throng of people and heard a voice calling, "Is this who you're looking for, ma'am?" Blond curls snapped into focus, and my heart stopped before it started beating again.

A young woman with dark hair was holding Ruth and waving to us. I began rushing toward her, and the woman set Ruth down and watched her toddle straight into my arms.

"Ruth Anne Darcy!" I babbled. "You mustn't run from Mama like that, darling. Thank you so much for catching her, miss. She's quick as lightning. I looked away for a moment, and she was gone."

The young woman smiled. She was pretty, with vivacious brown eyes and dark hair. She leaned down to talk to Maggie, and they proceeded to carry on a grown-up conversation while I tried to slow my pounding heartbeat. Through some pleasant small talk, I found out her name was Elizabeth Bennet, and she had just moved to town with her parents and sisters.

Suddenly, Maggie pulled away from my grasp, her excited "Unca!" ringing through the depot. I turned to see William several yards away, holding out his arms to the girls. I let Ruth down so she could follow her sister.

"I guess I should go. It was good to meet you Miss Bennet, and thank you again for catching Ruth."

"I hope to see you again soon." Elizabeth returned my friendly smile. "Goodbye Mrs…"

"Oh, I'm Georgiana. Georgiana Darcy." I was so flustered I'd forgotten to introduce myself.

When I approached William, he reached over and gave me a quick embrace. "Hello, Gi."

"Welcome home."

"I didn't expect you to bring the whole clan." He reached down and chucked Maggie's chin.

"We lost Ruth, but Elizabeth found her," Maggie piped up.

"What happened? Who found her?" he asked, his expression instantly stern.

"She got away while I was asking about your train. That nice young woman over there caught her before she got too far." I tried to discreetly point out Miss Bennet to him.

"Her name is Elizabeth, like my middle name," Maggie chimed in.

"Gi, you could have left the girls at home with Mrs. Reynolds."

"Well, William," I replied in exasperation, "I probably should have done that, but all they could talk about this morning was coming to get Unca. I didn't want to disappoint them." His terse tone, after I'd just had the scare of my life, was mighty irritating!

"Mmmph." He leaned over and gathered up Ruth with one arm.

I didn't take offense at his little grunt. I knew he would have brought them along too.

Maggie tried to take his suitcase and carry it for him, but it was as big as she was. He laughed.

"Here, Maggie Moo." He gave Ruth back to me and picked up the case in one hand and took Maggie's hand in the other. "How about you let me carry that big suitcase, and I'll hold your hand."

"All right." Maggie beamed up at him.

I took a deep breath to calm my nerves, and after seeing Maggie's adoration of her "Unca" for about the thousandth time, whispered a word of thanks for my big brother.

CHAPTER 5

DECEMBER 25, 1932

William's dark-clad form moved briskly around the car, scraping a thin film of ice off the windows. Wisps of breath rose in curls from his mouth. His cheeks were red from cold, and his eyes were bright. He looked almost...cheerful, for him anyway. Ruth turned in my arms, nestling into my bosom to finish out her nap. I laid my cheek against her soft, sweaty head. We were all heading to church, because Christmas was on Sunday this year.

Why did William insist that we go? It was out of character for the brother I knew in my youth. Back then, he had welcomed any excuse to skip church; it annoyed our parents to no end. So, why now, when we had the hustle and bustle of an early Christmas morning with two small children? That, combined with the cold, frosty weather, would usually be enough to keep him in front of the big stone fireplace at Pemberley.

Not that I minded. I liked getting out of the house now, mostly because people from the community had stopped looking askance at me. William had broadcast the news that my husband was gone, and I was going to make a home for my children in Meryton. I suspected that Sheriff Fitzwilliam also had a hand in presenting my story in a flattering light. Even the busybody matrons had stopped giving me the wary eye whenever I was in town.

I checked the back seat for Maggie, who was holding her doll and explaining to the toy where we were going and why. As if Dolly hadn't been to church almost every Sunday since August.

Since August. What had changed in August? Was it just that the girls and I had finally settled in and recuperated from our ordeal? Had William become a more regular churchgoer since I moved away? Was he simply thankful that I had returned? Was he praying for strength to deal with us all?

I chuckled to myself. His life had certainly changed with the addition of three females to his household. He was bearing up well under the upheaval of it all.

"Mama, will Elizabeth be at church today?" Maggie's serious face turned toward me.

"Probably, sweetheart. Why?"

"Last Sunday, she came to the nursery and read us a Christmas story. I liked that. I hope she reads another one today."

"I'm not sure if they will have the nursery during the sermon today —it being a holiday and all. Everyone who works the nursery will want to sit with their families, because it's Christmas."

"Oh. So, Elizabeth will sit with her sisters?"

"I would imagine she would," I replied absently, smoothing a wisp of hair from Ruth's cheek. She twitched in her sleep and swiped at her face with a chubby hand.

"I wish Elizabeth was my sister," Maggie said in a wistful voice.

I smiled indulgently. Maggie's hero worship of Elizabeth began the day we met her, when Elizabeth brought a wayward Ruth back to me at the train station. "Elizabeth is very nice, isn't she?"

"Yes, and she's very pretty. And she talks to me. And Unca likes her too."

I twisted around in the car seat. "What do you mean, darling?"

"Unca talked to Elizabeth at the ice cream party, and he watches her at church."

"Oh, really?"

Maggie nodded her head. "Unca should marry Elizabeth, and then she'd be my sister for real."

"Well, not exactly," I mused. "She'd be your aunt." Suddenly a thought occurred to me. "Maggie, you haven't said that to Elizabeth have you?"

Maggie's eyes opened wide in a guilty expression. "No Mama."

"That's good."

Maggie looked down. "But I did ask her if she wanted to come live at my house."

"What did she say?" I tried to hide my amusement.

"Just that she liked being my friend, but her mama and sisters needed her at home, like you need me."

I felt a warm tug at my heart for Elizabeth's masterful way of dealing with serious, sensitive Maggie. It reminded me of how William handled her.

Maggie went on, and her expression plainly showed that she was plotting. "But if Unca and her got married, she would *have* to come live with us, right?"

"Maggie..." I warned, using my stern mother's voice.

"But I won't say it, 'cause Unca would not like it if I asked her before he did."

She's absolutely right about that! "Good, and don't you dare say anything either, because that would embarrass Uncle, and Elizabeth too."

"But he wants to ask her," Maggie muttered, returning to her doll.

I decided we had probably discussed that topic long enough. Anyway, William had finished cleaning off the car windows and was climbing inside.

"Everybody ready to go?"

"Yes!" we said in unison, laughing at each other.

"No trips to the necessary room are necessary?"

"No!"

"All right then."

He started the car and off we went, as Maggie started up a chorus of "We Wish You a Merry Christmas."

"Sing it, Unca!" Maggie belted out, giggling. William looked at me with a self-deprecating smile and began to warble along with her in his rich baritone. I responded the only way I could. I joined in.

* * *

THE ORGAN PLAYED A VAGUELY familiar Christmas carol as the ushers gathered in front of the altar to receive the offering plates. William was among the four, his dark head bowed, solemn expression in place.

Sometimes I worried for him. He was pleasant, kind to me and to the girls—Maggie adored him—but he worked most of the time or was busy taking care of some legal tangle involving my bogus marriage or my children. Thankfully, a lot of that was over now, and we were all easing into the rhythm of farm life at Pemberley. William appeared content enough, and I knew he was glad to have us home, but he didn't seem happy. The last couple of months I had caught him acting restless, almost agitated as he went through the days. He had always been a great reader, but now when he sat down with a book, he laid it down in irritation after just a few minutes. He had also started taking long walks in the evenings. More than once, I saw him sitting in the loft of the barn until dusk, even as the cold autumn and winter weather set in.

William took his offering plate and directed Truman Long to the aisle beside him, while William took himself across the center of the church to the first aisle on the other side. It was an odd enough behavior that I watched him and tried to figure out what he was doing. The plate traveled down the front row and into Truman's waiting hand. The young man handed it back one row, and it returned to William. When it got there, however, Mrs. Owens had to nudge him to take it. Once again, he was distracted. But this time, I saw what had grabbed his attention. There, in the sixth row of the center section, near the aisle where William was passing the collection plate, sat Elizabeth Bennet. It was obvious what, or rather, who, had captivated his interest. Elizabeth was thumbing through a hymnal while she leaned over to whisper something to Charlotte Lucas. Her brilliant smile beamed in William's direction as she looked toward the front of the church. My gaze snapped back to him; he was struggling to keep his facial expression hidden. Other people might not notice, but I had spent most of my childhood following him everywhere he went. His eyes really were the windows to his soul, and they were alight with a warmth I had never seen before.

As the plate came down Elizabeth's pew, William watched her with a searing intensity. Only Lydia was between Elizabeth and William's waiting hand, so she would probably hand the plate to him herself. It was taking forever to reach the end of the row! Mr. Carleton took a month of Sundays to fish his money out of his pocket, but the plate finally resumed its journey. I held my breath, my eyes darting from the plate, to Elizabeth and back to William. It was almost there, and the suspense was absurdly unbearable. He took a deep breath and began to smile, but Elizabeth turned back to talk to Charlotte after briefly acknowledging him. His mouth snapped shut, and he stepped back. Disappointed, I exhaled the air I was holding.

I remembered Maggie's observation from the car. *"He watches her at church."* If anyone would notice anything unusual about William or Elizabeth, it would be the ever watchful Maggie. She worshipped both of them.

Was William in love with Elizabeth Bennet? When had he spent any time with her? There was the time she and Jane stayed at Netherfield last fall; he had visited there a few times while they were sewing dresses for Charles Bingley's aunts. Richard told me William danced with Elizabeth the night of the Bingleys' holiday party. Maggie said he talked to her at the ice cream social last fall. As I began putting the pieces together, a joyful feeling began in the pit of my stomach. My brother had finally had his heart touched by a woman.

I wondered if Elizabeth knew. Somehow I doubted it, from her lack of response to him. Of course, she would be thrilled, once he revealed himself. No woman in her right mind would ever refuse him.

So, what was holding him back? Why wasn't he courting her? She was young and pretty; if he waited too long, some other man might snap her up.

I stifled a giggle as I watched him almost trip over elderly Mr. Farnsworth on his way back from the altar. William apologized to the bewildered older man, and his cheeks flushed with embarrassment. He had run into poor Mr. Farnsworth because he was, of course, looking back at Elizabeth Bennet.

* * *

"RICHARD?" I whispered, looking over my shoulder and feeling slightly daring for using his first name. William had gone upstairs to read a bedtime story to Maggie, so I had a few minutes before he returned. I gestured for the sheriff to join me in the dining room.

"Miss Darcy? What are you…?"

"Quick, before William gets back. I need to ask you something."

He stepped into the room, and I pulled the French doors closed behind him.

"Has William mentioned anyone to you lately?"

He looked confused.

"A lady, I mean. Has he talked about courting anyone?"

Richard shook his head, still looking at me with a baffled expression.

"I think he's sweet on Elizabeth."

"The Bennet girl?"

I nodded.

"Well, I'll be… I never would've guessed."

"You'll encourage him, won't you? Without being obvious, of course."

"You *want* your brother to jump the broom?"

"Yes! Why wouldn't I?"

"Some women would want to keep their place as mistress of the house—'specially this house." He looked around the room.

My smile dimmed. "No, I have no interest in being mistress of this house, certainly not at the expense of my brother's happiness. Wouldn't it be wonderful if he found someone to love?"

"Maybe it would, but I'm not gettin' in the middle of that mess. I'm no matchmaker, ma'am."

"Of course not. But if he were to ask you, or there was a chance for him to see her, you'll make it easy for him, won't you? I don't think she knows, and she never will if he doesn't do anything beyond staring at her from the church pew and asking her to dance once a year at the Bingleys' Christmas party."

Richard laughed. "Well, I'll do what I can, for your sake."

"Thank you." I suddenly realized I was alone with him. "Umm, yes… well…"

"Shall we open the door now?" His voice held a touch of amusement at my awkwardness.

"Yes." I breathed out in an uncontrolled rush, reaching for the handle. He reached for the handle too, and our hands touched over top of it. I drew mine back as if it burned.

"Excuse me, sorry," I babbled.

"No, excuse me, Miss Matchmaker." He chuckled and opened the door just as William was descending the stairs.

CHAPTER 6

The soft, red, leather book still felt foreign in my hands. My old diary was one of the only surviving relics of the girl I once was. Girlish musings littered the first half of the journal—simple things about music and books, friends and foes from school. If only my life could be that simple again. Now, I felt aged and brittle, like the yellowed pages of this journal. My smooth, lacy script, the product of the best private schooling money could buy, covered the paper. The words I had written there today were a stark contrast to everything that had come before:

I found this journal when I was going through some of my things last week. The last time I wrote in it I was fourteen years old. Now I'm twenty-two. No longer a girl. No longer an innocent. I'm a fallen woman—a mother, a sister that is well on her way to becoming a burden on her brother for the rest of her life. I am sad, lonely, and looking down the barrel of another sad, lonely year.

I think I'm in love. Really in love this time, not some silly infatuation that promises escape and excitement. He smiles and I feel contentment. He laughs and I feel joy. I feel his voice hum in the center of my chest. But he would not want me. I'm used up, broken, afraid, thin and gaunt, haggard. I'm damaged.

Then again...

I'm also a young woman with pretty gray eyes and a nice smile—a mother, a sister who wants her brother to find his happiness. In a small corner of my heart, I guess I'm still hopeful. I'm a survivor. I want to show my daughters how to live with courage. I want happiness of my own. In the depths of my despair, I promised myself that I would not live in fear anymore.

So, happiness will be my New Year's resolution, and I will record my path to it in this journal. My joie de vivre does not depend on my trust fund, on my accomplishments, on William, on the girls, on anyone or anything. I find joy in all those things, but the happiness? No, it comes from inside me, and no matter what happens in my life, I can let myself be happy. Like Richard does. Despite all his hardships, he has let himself find a life worth living. He has so much to teach me, and how I want to learn it! More than learning though, I want to share it all with him.

But first, I must banish my fear...

"You look quite serious for a Sunday afternoon, and it's a holiday too."

I jumped at the sound of my brother's deep voice and put a hand over my heart. "Mercy! You scared me."

"I'm sorry. You were engrossed in your book, and you looked so far away. Are you all right, Gigi?"

I snapped the book shut so quickly I knew he couldn't have read it. "Yes, thank you, I'm all right. I found this journal and decided I would start keeping one again." A cautious smile crept across my lips. "I was making New Year's resolutions."

William seemed pleased with that. He came into the parlor and sat on the sofa in front of the writing desk. "That's a wonderful idea. I'm glad you're thinking about the future again. You've come a long way since that spring afternoon you arrived back home."

"Well, it has been over a year."

"Your smile is back." He hesitated. "Sometimes, though, you still seem unhappy."

My gaze dropped to the floor lest he see the uneasiness I felt. My budding feelings for Richard were not up for discussion at this point, but the other things? Well, maybe I *could* tell him those. After all, we were a family again. "It's still hard to take sometimes, the betrayal, the guilt and shame of it all."

He interrupted me almost immediately. "That scoundrel isn't worth a minute of your time, much less your tears."

"I know." I sighed, remembering he had said this many times before.

William's eyes were almost black with anger. "I wish you'd never laid eyes on him. I wish he'd never been born."

A resigned sadness bubbled up from deep inside me. "Even though he gave us Maggie and Ruth?"

William stopped short and shut his mouth with a snap.

"See? It's not so cut and dry, is it? When I think about it now, I suppose George really tried—at the beginning—to be a good husband. At times, he could be very sweet and charming. After all, there was a reason I ran off with him. But circumstances like his past, and my ignorance about the world—all those obstacles were just too much for a weak man like him to overcome. I'm not making excuses for him, because there were also the drinking binges, the disappearing for weeks at a time, and of course, the violence. He chose to do those things. I don't know how it could have been if he had behaved differently. If he hadn't been married when he met me. But he killed my love for him the day he hit Maggie."

"Some women watch that happen year after year, and don't have the strength to do what you did."

"Some women don't have a brother who is kind and willing to take them in. They don't have a place to go." I laid my hand on his, resting on the back of the couch, and pressed it. "Thank God for you, William. I know I do, every single day."

"It wasn't a big heroic gesture. You all are my family, the only family I have. I'm happy to take care of you."

"Well"—I replied briskly, sensing his discomfort with my praise —"you're my hero, and Ruth's hero, and especially Maggie's hero."

He looked sheepish and grinned. "Did I tell you what the little imp said to me the other day?"

"No, what?"

"Told me I needed a wife, so she could have an auntie and cousins."

I sputtered with laughter. Maggie had apparently been busy this week, presenting her case. "What did you tell her?" His cheeks had gotten noticeably redder; he had probably not meant to tell me that.

"I said it was not her concern."

"Did she have a candidate for this position of the 'wife'?"

He continued looking at the ground, a faraway expression on his face.

"Perhaps, Elizabeth Bennet?"

His head snapped up in shock. "How did you know?"

"How did I know Maggie suggested it? Or how did I know you'd been considering it? Don't look at me like that. It's written all over your face whenever you're near her."

"It is not!"

"It is to me."

"Hmmph. Good lord, Gi. I hardly know her."

"So, get to know her better. Ask to court her."

"She won't want me. I'm so much older than her."

"Trust me. A woman can easily fall in love with a man who's older than she is." *I'm living proof of that.* "And you're quite the catch, you know."

"Do you think so?"

"I know so. She would be a fool to reject you. Think how much you could enrich her life—and I don't mean just financial security, either."

"Maybe she would overlook the difference in our ages, if there were… other benefits."

I couldn't help a giggle. "Goodness, William, you're not a piece of farm equipment."

"No, but she's very practical. She thinks about things carefully. I've seen it."

"If you want her, ask her. Life is short, Brother. Don't wait and have regrets later."

"Maybe… We'll see." He stood up, obviously finished with this line of conversation. "I'll let you get back to your journal."

"All right."

He stopped at the doorway, a serious expression on his face. "Gigi?"

"Yes?"

"I see what you mean, about Wickham giving us Maggie and Ruth. I never thought about it before, but perhaps I could show him mercy if I had to, for their sakes. I could live and let live, because he's one of the reasons they're here."

"I think that would be good for your soul. Your friend Richard says that bitterness poisons the spirit."

He nodded once and exited the room.

I looked over what I had written earlier.

…banish my fear

I picked up my pen and wrote with a flourish:

Bitterness poisons the spirit. – R.F.

"You're absolutely right, Sheriff," I whispered, drawing my finger lovingly over his words.

CHAPTER 7

FEBRUARY 14, 1933

My heart was pounding the moment I entered the sheriff's office. The doorbell rang out through the small room, announcing my presence, and I drew a deep breath as Richard looked up from his papers. Myrna, the dispatcher, was on her lunch break, so he was minding the front office. When he realized I was the visitor, he stood so abruptly his chair scraped the worn pine floor.

"Well, good afternoon." His open, friendly smile lit his face, while he took in my appearance with what I hoped was an appreciative glance. I had taken special effort, dressed in my most becoming clothes, tried to exude confidence, but the wringing of my hands probably gave away my nervousness.

"What can I do for you, Miss Darcy?"

His voice sent a very pleasant shiver down my spine. I swallowed hard and tried to answer in a clear, self-assured voice. "Good afternoon. May I speak with you a minute, Sheriff?"

"Of course."

Banish my fear, banish my fear. "In private?" I glanced around the room at the two deputies standing with coffee in their hands, their curiosity obvious. A prickly heat crept up my chest and burned my cheeks.

"We can go in my office, if you'd like. Mercer, mind the phone, won't you?"

"Sure thing, boss."

Richard opened the door and held it while I stepped inside. He inhaled sharply as I passed him in the doorway, and a shower of sparks crackled over my skin from stepping so close to him. He shut the door behind us.

No fear, Georgiana. I squared my shoulders and took another deep breath before I turned to face him.

His expression immediately shifted from pleased to concerned. "Are you all right, honey?"

My heart fluttered at his use of the endearment, although he was the kind of Southern gentleman who called women honey all the time. "Oh, yes. I'm fine, wonderful, in fact. I suppose you've heard about William and Elizabeth getting married?"

"Yes, he asked me to stand up with him."

"It is marvelous news, just what I wanted—as I'm sure you remember."

His lips twitched in a little grin. "Yes, I remember."

I stood looking at him for several seconds, while my heart hammered out a rapid cadence. A happy sigh escaped me; how I loved that secretive little grin of his!

"Georgiana?"

"Yes?"

"Why did you come see me?"

It was a struggle to focus on my purpose for being there. Even though he stood a good five feet away from me, being alone with him made this conversation seem so intimate. "Oh, yes. That. I need some advice, from someone who knows William." I paced back and forth, wringing my hands. "I'm very happy for them. I don't think she knows yet, but she's about to catch almost the best bachelor around."

"That goes without saying."

"I have been thinking quite a bit about what life will be like at Pemberley after he marries. I'm concerned that having another family living in his house will be a detriment to his marriage. If he is trying to be a father to my girls, and a companion for me, he will not learn to be the husband he should be. We will present too many distractions. Newlyweds need time and freedom to build their life together."

"Yes," Richard said warily, lifting his brow. It was obvious he could see where this was going, and he wished I wouldn't tell him the rest. He knew as well as I did, that William was going to throw a fit about what I was planning to do.

The next words came out in a rush. "I've decided to move out of the big house." I looked in his eyes to find my courage, and there it was. "Now, before you tell me about why I shouldn't—"

"I would never tell you that you shouldn't."

"Really?"

"Perhaps you should just finish what you came here to say."

"Yes. Well, William needs his home back so he can start his family, but I don't want to leave Pemberley entirely. It's my home too. I own part of it, and I can't think of a better place to raise my girls. It would be very hard on them to be too far away from William, and it would be hard for him as well. I would hate for him to feel guilty for pursuing his own happiness and think I left because he decided to take a wife. So, this is what I've planned. Mrs. Reynolds and I have been down to look at the foreman's cottage. Do you remember it?"

"Yes, 'bout half a mile down the road from the house, isn't it?"

I nodded. "It is in some disrepair, but I think we could be comfortable if some renovations were made. Then, William and Elizabeth can begin their life together, and I can move on with mine."

"Makes sense to me. So, what do you want me to do?"

"I have no idea how to tell if the cottage really is livable, so I need a knowledgeable opinion on that. If it is, I need some references for renovating—putting in electricity, plumbing, that sort of thing. You updated your parents' house, didn't you? I thought you mentioned it once."

"I did, a few years back." He paused, uncertainty clouding his face. "Your brother is going to be upset about this—madder than a hornet that we kept it from him."

"I'm not going to keep it from him." My chin automatically lifted in defiance. "He's planning a honeymoon trip to Nashville for a few days. I'll tell him when he returns. I don't think it's fair to burden him with this while he's preparing for the wedding. So, I guess I'm asking for your discretion as well, just until I can talk to him about it."

"He would let you live at the big house forever, if you wanted."

"I know that, and he will probably try to talk me out of this, but I can't…" My eyes filled with tears.

"Can't what?"

His empathetic look nearly made me lose my composure. I struggled to put my thoughts into words.

"I'm grateful to my brother. I know very well what he has done for me. He saved my life, and the lives of my children. I can never repay him for that, only accept his gift with grace. But I deserve my own life, my own family—and so does he. I can't have that if I stay under his wing, and unless I force this on him, his guilt will never allow him to let me go. I'm doing this for him, but I'm also doing it for my sake. Is that selfish?"

Richard sat down slowly in the old ladder back chair behind his desk. The wooden joints creaked and groaned as he tilted the chair on its back legs. His stunned expression turned thoughtful. Unable to meet his gaze any longer, I looked down and fiddled with my hands as I often did when I was nervous. I was scared, he could probably see that, but I was also determined, and I hoped he could see that too. Standing up to the brother I revered almost as much as a father took some serious moxie.

"No, it's not selfish. It's probably one of the most selfless things I've ever witnessed." His voice held a quiet, reverent tone. "You're a good woman, Georgiana."

I looked at him and felt the faint fluttering of hope.

He cleared his throat. "So, to answer your question. Yes, I'll help you. I know a man over in Brighton who does this kind of work for a reasonable price. He's worked on my house, and he's a fine and honest gentleman. If you'd like, I'll ask him to meet us out there—when, do you think?"

"Next Monday will be perfect. I'm not planning to move until after William and Elizabeth return." I leaned over and laid my hand on his forearm, resting on the arm of the chair.

"I'll see what I can arrange then."

"Richard, thank you! You've been such a good friend to us, to me." His eyes were riveted on my hand, and I pulled back, scarcely believing I'd had the nerve to touch him.

His easy chuckle filled the room, and my awkwardness evaporated. "You're welcome. I hope I don't end up on the other end of your brother's fist."

"I won't let that happen."

"I have your protection then?" he teased.

"You have my word."

"Fair enough."

There was a long pause.

"Well, then, goodbye."

"Goodbye."

I exited the office, wishing I knew what was going on behind those intense blue eyes.

CHAPTER 8

MARCH 19, 1933

"How did the old boy take it when you said you were moving out?" Richard stepped up on the second rung of the ladder to apply masking tape around the window frame.

"He is worried about the girls, I think, especially Maggie. He didn't say much, just put on that famous scowl of his, but I know he's thinking she won't adjust well to more changes. I wish he'd realize this is nothing like when we came home, and she's so much happier now. I think she's going to do just fine."

"I'm sure you're right, Little Mama." He winked at me, and I felt my face go white as my heart stopped, and then go red as the blood thundered in my ears.

I turned back to the wall I was painting to hide my flushed face. "What surprised me was Elizabeth's reaction. She almost asked me not to go. Wanted to make sure I knew we were welcome to live at Pemberley." I stopped and turned toward Richard. "Don't you think that's a little odd?"

Richard shrugged. "Maybe. I'm sure it's a big change for her, not just being a wife and…everything that goes with that," he said a little awkwardly. "But she's used to a house full o'girls, and Pemberley is currently a house full o'girls. That big old place is a lot of room for just two people and a housekeeper."

Richard pulled out his pocket knife to jimmy open a paint can. "It oughta stay that empty for a while, in my opinion. They need some time to settle in."

"Don't you like her?"

"Miss Bennet? I mean, Mrs. Darcy? Oh yeah, I like her fine, but I'm afraid William might've rushed it a little. I thought he'd court her for a while and then ask her to get married, but he went straight for the 'I do's'. It's unlike him, to jump in with both feet like that."

"I guess when you know you've met your true love, you don't want to wait." I studied him carefully, trying to gauge his reaction to my words.

He smiled. "You believe in love at first sight, do ya?"

"Perhaps. Do you?"

He laughed softly. "I believe in lust at first sight. Love comes with time."

"Oh." Another spell of awkwardness, and another reason for me to look away.

"Didn't mean to embarrass you, honey."

"It's all right."

He shook his head in remorse. "I forget, sometimes, that you're a lady."

What? My head snapped up to meet his gaze head on. I was sure my expression held complete shock, and perhaps a touch of anger as well.

His eyes opened wide. "Oh no! I didn't mean it like that."

My brow drew into an automatic furrow, and I narrowed my eyes at him, giving him my best Darcy scowl.

"I'm sorry. Them words just came roarin' out, afore they went through my brain. What I meant to say is—you and me, we can talk about most anything, and we know each other well. It isn't like with other ladies, where I'm obliged to watch everything I say. We're friends, good friends, and I…" He fished around awkwardly for something else to say. "I'm making this worse, aren't I?"

His stuttered words and flustered face made it impossible to stay annoyed with him. "You're forgiven. I know what you mean—I can tell you almost anything, but then, you already know everything about me anyway."

His blue eyes softened. "Not the important things."

"What important things?"

"Oh, like your favorite cake, or what subject you liked best in school, or your favorite color."

"Chocolate, history and blue," I replied with a little smile.

"Duly noted, ma'am. I already know you like lavender soap…" He stopped suddenly.

When my head tilted and my expression grew curious, he cleared his throat and looked back at the wall. "Did Mrs. Darcy like the perfume you got her for a wedding present?"

"Yes, she did. Thank you again for driving down and picking it up for me. I really wanted to give it to her before they married."

"Never felt so out of place in my life as when I went in that perfume shop."

I chuckled, the image of my small-town sheriff standing in the perfume store with his hat in his hand and shifting his weight from one foot to the other. "Well, my sister-in-law and I thank you. And my brother too, I would imagine."

Richard sobered. After several seconds, he went on. "Your brother's feelings are deep, and he rarely shows them to anyone. I hope he learns to trust Mrs. Darcy enough to let her see that side of him, and that she's worthy of his trust. 'Cause he's good and caught in her net, that's for sure."

"Still another reason for me to set up house here. They need to depend on each other so that trust will grow, and not depend on me or the girls for company."

"Mmm."

I wiped my brow with my forearm, careful not to get paint from my fingers in my hair. "Thank you for helping out today. This will go a lot faster with two brushes."

"I'm glad to do it, but you know, you could have hired a house painter."

"Oh, I will, for the outside. But I thought I could do a few of the rooms on my own. It just turned into a bigger job than I thought."

"Where's them little girls this morning?"

"Mrs. Reynolds is watching them for me. I'd never be able to keep Ruth out of the paint. It would end up everywhere, except on the walls."

Richard smiled and nodded in agreement. "So, once you move into this palace, do you have any plans then?"

"Nothing that unusual. Just raising my girls, gardening, helping on the farm where I'm needed. Watching over my brother and taking care of nieces and nephews, hopefully."

"Give them some time to get to know each other first, Auntie."

We both laughed and fell silent again, listening to the swish of the paint brushes against the wall. It was so easy being with him, so pleasant.

Richard kept his eyes firmly in front of him. "No young man waiting in the wings?"

"No." The word rushed out of my mouth, in a sharper tone than I intended.

"Ah."

We continued painting into the awkward silence left by Richard's question, but he persisted.

"Because you haven't found the right young man, I'm assuming?"

I chose my words carefully. "I haven't sworn off men. It's just…"

"Just what?"

I dipped my paint brush in the can and wiped the excess against the rim. "I'm also realistic. I know I'm hardly a prize for a young bachelor—a fallen woman with two small daughters." Shock clouded his handsome face at my assessment, but he said nothing, so I went on.

"Most men want to have children of their own, not raise some other man's."

"There is more to a marriage than having children. You might be surprised. Some young feller would be mighty lucky to have you for his wife."

I forced out a brief chuckle, but the lack of humor was evident. "Well, I guess there's always my trust fund. A young man might be interested in that."

"Don't be cynical, Georgiana," he said quietly. "It doesn't suit you."

My cheeks burned with shame. "You're right, of course. I have much to be thankful for."

"You can feel gratitude and still live angry, but it's not good for your soul. You can trust me on that."

My affection for him shone through my smile, I was sure. "How does the sheriff of a little county in Kentucky get to be such a wise philosopher?"

"Just livin' life, honey," he said with a wink and a grin.

"I can see why my brother trusts you. You've been a good friend to him—something else I'm very grateful for."

"We've helped each other."

We carried on in companionable silence, laughing when we bumped foreheads as we dipped our brushes in the paint can.

"How's Jerry working out for you? Any problems with the renovations?"

"Oh no. Mr. McElwain is very professional. I've been pleased with his work so far."

"Good to hear. I'm not surprised though. He's a good egg. Who did he get to do the electrical wiring? He had to hire someone from Bowling Green for my house."

I dipped my brush. "His son did the wiring actually."

"His son? He can't be grown already, can he?"

"He certainly can," I answered, amused. "He got his electrical training up East somewhere, but now he's come back to work for his father. Dan told me his father is grooming him to take over the business in a few years."

"Dan?"

"Mr. McElwain's son."

"I remember when 'Dan' was 'little Danny', runnin' around and puttin' frogs in his sister's shoes just to hear her squeal."

I laughed. "Yes, he told me some funny stories about growing up with four sisters. Of course, none of those stories painted him as the mischievous one."

"I would imagine not." Richard frowned. "How long did it take him to wire up this place? I imagine it wasn't a very big job."

"Oh no, it was over a week. That's why we couldn't paint until now."

"A week? I wouldn't think it would take that long."

"That's what his father said, but Dan told him he wanted to go slowly and be especially thorough, because I'm a woman living here alone with little ones. Very chivalrous of him, don't you think?"

Richard snorted. "Very." His voice sounded a little irritated, although I couldn't imagine why. "It's not as if your brother wasn't just up the road."

I only smiled a little.

We continued painting in silence, each lost in our own thoughts until the wall was finished. I laid my paintbrush on the can and arched my back to stretch it. I lifted my arms above my head and closed my eyes for a second. When I opened them, I saw him out of the corner of my eye. He swallowed hard and turned away.

"I guess this about does it. Do you want to come up to the house for something cold to drink?" I tried to give him my most inviting smile. It had been a long time since I tried to flirt with someone, and I was not very good at it.

He drew a deep breath and sighed. "I'll give you a ride up to the house, but then I really should get back to town."

"Oh." My smile deflated. Then I brightened with another thought. "You'll come for lunch on Sunday, won't you?"

"You think the newlyweds will want company so soon?"

"It's been over a month since you were up at the house. *I* want your company, and I'm sure they will too. So, the invitation stands, Sheriff."

"If you insist." He caught my gaze and held it.

"I do insist," I said, slightly breathless. After a long moment, I turned, keenly aware of his eyes on me as I walked in front of him toward the truck. A pleasant arc raced up my spine to warm the back of my neck. Now, I would be counting the days until Sunday.

CHAPTER 9

APRIL 1, 1933

It was one of those blissful spring days when the balmy air was just beginning to warm the earth. Everything smelled new—budding trees, new grass. The jonquils I'd planted along the path were blooming and nodding in the breeze. I turned my attention to the embroidery in my lap.

"Whatcha makin' there, Miss Darcy?" Dan McElwain gestured toward my current project with his glass.

"This? Oh." I held it up for him to see. "It's a pillowcase."

"Very beautiful." He sent me an indulgent smile, the way a young man smiles when he couldn't care less about something, but wants to compliment and flatter.

"I haven't done embroidery in a while," I said, looking back at my lap. "The last few years I've done a lot more mending and sewing."

He nodded and smiled vacantly.

"And knitting. I've done some knitting," I said, chuckling softly at the empty look on his face. "And you have no interest in discussing this, do you?"

He had the good manners to look a little sheepish. "Don't know much about needlework, I suppose." He kept smiling though. "Be like you trying to talk about wires and volts and such."

"Point taken," I answered in a good-natured way.

"We'll have to find us a topic in common," he said, leaning forward. "Like…"

"Yes?"

"Like…"

I grinned at him. "You can't think of one, can you?"

"Give me a minute," he protested. "I can do it."

"Don't work too hard on it. It's Saturday afternoon."

"That it is, that it is."

I picked up the embroidery and completed another stitch or two while he watched. It was a comfortable silence. He sat there, with a glass of tea propped on his knee and his arm draped across the back of the glider like he owned the place—one of those cocky young men that I used to find so appealing. He truly was a sweetheart, though.

The sound of a car door slam alerted me that I had another visitor.

"I've got it." He grinned mischievously. "We could talk about President Roosevelt's New Deal."

I laughed out loud, shaking my head.

"Or going to see King Kong at the picture show, maybe?"

I was distracted by the new arrival, but I still heard the hopeful tone in his voice. Dan sat up straight when he saw my company approaching. My heart fluttered, trapped against my ribcage, and a smile burst from my lips.

"Richard! I wasn't expecting to see you today."

"Apparently not," he mumbled tersely. I sank against my chair, taken aback by his grumpy tone.

Dan stood up and extended his hand. "I don't think we've met, sir. I'm Dan McElwain."

Richard shook his hand and sized the young man up. "Oh, we've met, son. You were just too young to remember. Richard Fitzwilliam. Your daddy and I go way back."

"Sheriff Fitzwilliam? I do remember you now. My father speaks very highly of you. How are you, sir?"

"Doin' well, thank you." Richard looked up at the house. "I thought you finished the wiring on Miss Darcy's place already."

"I did finish it, oh…couple weeks ago, wasn't it?" He looked at me for confirmation, and I nodded.

"You in between jobs then? I'd think there would be plenty of work in Brighton."

"No, we generally don't work on Saturday afternoons." He stole a look over at me. "So, I came to check on Miss Darcy. Make sure everything was working the way it should."

"I see." Richard nodded toward the drink on the little outdoor table. "And got a tall glass of Miss Darcy's iced tea for your trouble." He turned his attention toward me and gave me an almost accusatory look. "Where's them little girls?"

"Napping," I returned, bewildered and a little put off by his manner.

Richard's voice grew rough. "Your brother here?"

"I assume he's up at the house. I'm not living there any longer, so I don't know for sure." I stared at this man and wondered where my sweet, gentle friend had gone. I didn't know this stern fellow at all. He stared back. I'm not sure what he was trying to convey, but for once, he seemed unable to alter his face into his usual lazy grin.

Dan cleared his throat. "Well, I suppose I should get going. My mother will have supper ready soon, and she'll squawk mighty loud if I'm not there on time."

"Goodbye, Danny. Nice to see you again." Richard chimed in quickly, keeping his eyes on me. It was unnerving.

"You too, Sheriff. I'll have to tell my dad I saw one of his old buddies. He'll get a kick out of that." He reached over and handed me his glass, along with an earnest smile. "Thank you for the tea, Miss Darcy. You make sure to call me if you have any trouble, ya hear?"

"I'm sure everything will be fine, but thank you."

Richard and I stood together and watched the young man head out to his truck in silence.

"Now, what was that all about?" Richard asked after the truck drove away in a cloud of red dust.

"Well, good afternoon to you too. Won't you sit down? Can I get you anything? Or would you rather launch right into the interrogation, Sheriff?"

Surprise raced across his features. I was a little surprised myself at my reaction, and miffed, and maybe a little defensive too.

"My apologies, Miss Darcy," he said formally. I half-expected a courtly little bow. "As your brother's friend, I just want to make sure that young man wasn't imposing on you. You are out here all alone, after all."

So that was it, more overprotection, as if William wasn't bad enough! I thought Richard understood me better than this, after all those conversations we'd had since I decided to move out of the big house.

"I know my history with men may not suggest it, but I'm not completely foolish. Dan McElwain is not a stranger, and I didn't invite him inside. Besides, he's harmless."

"Harmless, you say?" Richard's lips twitched. "I don't know about that. Now, I wonder why a strapping young stallion like that would drive all the way over here from Brighton on a Saturday afternoon? Maybe to spend some time with a pretty girl?"

My mouth hung open in shock. "Richard! You surely don't think he—"

"I know how young men think." He gave me a wistful smile. "I was one once."

I rolled my eyes, exasperated with him. "But you don't know how I think, and I can assure you that you don't know what you're talking about. Dan McElwain is not interested in me." *Well, maybe he is, a little bit. But I'm not interested in him.* I turned and went in the house, calling irritably over my shoulder. "There's iced tea, if you'd like a glass."

After a tense silence, he replied, "I'll take you up on that." As he followed me in the house though, I heard him say, "Not interested, my foot. I'm no April Fool."

CHAPTER 10

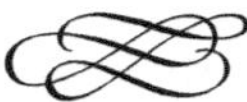

*E*lizabeth reached into the cabinet and retrieved a couple of plates. "Here, Georgiana, let me pack up some chicken and biscuits for your supper. I'll put some pie in there too." She reached into a drawer and pulled out a roll of aluminum foil. "Goodness, it's such a luxury to have tin foil to use on leftovers. I'd forgotten how handy it was." She paused and gave me a sidelong glance. "Should I pack enough for Sheriff Fitzwilliam too?"

My stomach turned over. Did she suspect something? And if so, would she tell William? And would William tell Richard?

"I thought he might stay to supper with you and the girls."

"Oh. Well, perhaps." Eager to get the conversation topic away from a certain blue-eyed sheriff, I changed the subject. "You seem to be settling in well. Do you like being married?"

Elizabeth smiled, apparently willing to let the subject of my sheriff go, for now. "I'm learning my way around. It's a lovely home."

"I've always thought so." I paused. "How is William doing since we moved to the cottage?"

"He doesn't say much, but I know he misses you. That first week after you left, I would catch him around bedtime, standing at the door to Maggie's room."

"Oh dear."

"When I asked him about it, he said that he used to read to Maggie at night. I knew it was part of his routine, and he seemed out of sorts without it, so that's when I suggested I read to *him* before bedtime."

"Really?"

"Mm-hmm. I had just started re-reading *The Adventures of Tom Sawyer*, so we began with that one." She got out a paper bag to set the plates in. "I think we'll do *Persuasion* next."

"Well, I think it's wonderful that you all are making new traditions with just the two of you, husband and wife."

Elizabeth smiled a little strangely. "It's still odd to think of myself as someone's wife."

I took the bag off the counter and gave Elizabeth a one-armed embrace. "You let me know if you need anything. I'm just down the road."

"I will, and thank you."

"I'll see you sometime this week, I'm sure."

The torrential rain had slacked off, but the gray clouds just over the hill suggested that another downpour was on its way. Richard stuck his head in the kitchen door.

"Georgiana, if you want to beat that next rain shower, you might want to come on now."

We walked into the foyer, and Elizabeth helped Ruth put her arms in her jacket. "Do you want me to get you an umbrella?"

"No, don't bother with that. We won't melt."

Maggie was saying her goodbyes to her Unca. Her little arms were entwined around his neck as he held her against his shoulder. "See you tomorrow?" she asked.

"I've got to plant that field tomorrow if the weather's good, sweetheart."

"But you'll see Unca real soon," Elizabeth said, patting Maggie's back. William lowered her to the ground gently, and I took her hand, transferring the bag to the hand that was holding Ruth.

"Here, hand me that one," Richard volunteered, reaching out to take Ruth from me. "All right, everyone ready?"

We disappeared into the gathering dusk and strode to the truck, peeking out from under our jacket hoods. I hustled Maggie in front of me and put her in the middle of the seat. I followed her in, and Richard handed Ruth in to sit on my lap. He had no sooner climbed in, when the clouds opened, sending a deluge of rain down from the heavens.

"Mercy!" I exclaimed.

"Muh-see!" Ruth repeated, and we all laughed.

"Richard, can you even see to drive this thing?"

"Yep, I know the way by heart." He smiled at me, and I was toasty warm despite the cool evening air.

We drove slowly down the hill and were just turning into the gravel drive at the cottage, when there was a loud clunk and the truck lurched to one side.

"Uh oh," Maggie piped up in a warning tone.

"Uh oh is right, sugar bean. I think we just went off that little culvert at the bottom of the drive." He shifted gears and tried to back out, but the tires spun in vain. Richard looked over at me and caught me biting my lip to keep a straight face.

"Go ahead, you can laugh if you want. I'm stuck," he admitted. "Why don't you run the young'uns in the house? I'll try to work my way out."

"Come in once you get the truck out, and I'll make you a cup of coffee. I don't want you driving back all cold and wet." I turned to my daughter. "Ready Maggie? On your mark, get set, go!" I pushed open the door and got out, turning to drag Maggie out by the elbow.

She squealed when the rain hit her. "Oooh, Mama! It's cold!"

"Hurry then!"

It took Richard quite a while to get the truck out. He finally had to wedge a fallen branch under the tire for some traction, and then he managed to drive out and up to the cottage. He took off his boots at the door and ventured inside.

"Hello?"

"I left you a towel there in the kitchen," I said as I walked from the parlor to the hall. "Let me get these girls in the bed. I'll put some coffee on when I'm done. I left you a plate of supper in the kitchen, too."

When I joined him about ten minutes later, I had changed my damp dress. My hair, darker when wet, hung down my back and curled around my face. It was not the sophisticated look I was going for when I dressed this morning! I tried in vain to dry my hair one more time, rubbing my wet locks between the ends of the towel but to no avail. I sighed, giving up on my appearance for the evening, and smiled over at Richard, who was sitting at the table and looking at me a little slack-jawed. *I must look worse than I thought.* I moved around the kitchen, gathering coffee and the "fixins", as he called the cream and sugar. While the coffee brewed, I sat down at my little kitchen dinette.

"Are you still cold? We can wring your shirt out and hang it up to dry some."

He looked aghast at the suggestion. "No matter. It'll be fine."

"Don't be silly, Richard. You're soaked through. I'll get you something to wrap around you if you're cold." Without waiting for an answer, I disappeared into the other room and returned, bringing an extra towel. "There, you can step into the bathroom, if you feel modest." My lips twitched in amusement. He retreated and came out with the towel hanging over his shoulders. I tried not to look at the wiry bare torso underneath.

"I hung the shirt on the side of the tub. Mmm. Coffee smells good."

"Here, I'll get you a cup." I turned and poured the coffee with shaking hands. Suddenly, there was a new tension in the room.

"You take your coffee with cream and sugar, don't you?"

"Yes, ma'am, thank you."

I set the cup down in front of him and turned back to fix my own. "It was fun, teaching Elizabeth to play Rook this afternoon."

"Yep, she learnt quick."

"William is crazy about her, but she's harder to read." I sat down across the corner from him, warming both hands on my cup.

"Mmm." He sipped his coffee and looked around the kitchen. "Electricity's working well."

"Yes. No problems at all."

"I'll let Jerry know. No sense in little Danny driving over from Brighton to *check* on you next Saturday." Richard's voice held the hint of a tease, but I was in no mood for it. I got up abruptly and went to the sink.

"I've told you, I have no interest in Dan McElwain," I said, feeling a bit cross. "Why do you keep bringing it up?"

"I apologize." He stared at his coffee cup and thoughtfully turned it one complete rotation before picking it back up and taking another sip. "I guess I didn't like him sniffin' around here." He paused. "But you shouldn't mind me, I'm sure he's a fine fella."

There was a long pause while I considered his words. Was it possible he teased me about Dan because he was…jealous? Could it be that he felt about me the same way I did about him? My heart began to pound. The air crackled around me while I formed and released the next words, almost against my will.

"Dan McElwain is a nice boy, but I left girlhood behind a long time ago—prematurely perhaps. I can't go back there ever again." I warmed his coffee up and set the pot down on the table. Standing beside him, I raised one end of his towel to dry his hair. His eyes slid closed, and a tiny smile crossed his lips. In an instant, the room seemed unbearably warm.

My voice was soft, hesitant—far away sounding, as if it came from someone else. "I don't need a boy." I dropped the towel back in place, leaving my hand on his shoulder. He turned and looked up at me. I lifted my other hand and traced his stubbly jaw with shaking fingers. "I need a man. This man."

His expression became instantly serious. "Georgiana, what are you saying?"

I withdrew my hand and looked at him in dismay. A tide of mortification rose and struck me with a sudden, devastating force. I cast my eyes down at the floor, my cheeks flaming hot. "I—I'm sorry," I stammered. "I didn't intend to say that. I'm so embarrassed." My next words were muffled by my fingers covering my face. "I thought you might feel the same way. I'm so tired of hiding my heart, and—oh, it doesn't matter." I turned around and went to the sink to wash my cup, desperate for something to occupy my hands. I went on in a shaky voice, trying to hold in my tears. "Just, please, don't tell William. I couldn't bear him knowing that I threw myself at you like that." I heard the chair scrape the floor and felt him behind me before he spoke. He lightly placed his hands on my shoulders.

"Darling girl, I won't say anything. But are you sure you're not confusing affection for a friend with a love that's between a man and a woman? I'm almost old enough to be your father, more than fifteen years older than you. You're young and beautiful, and you deserve a man who's young like you are, not some old broken-down widower past his prime, like me."

I whirled around, suddenly angry. "Don't hide behind your age or mine! Love can transcend those years. If you don't love me, tell me so. I can accept that, but don't try to make me feel better with flimsy excuses. Be honest with me. I told you before, I'm realistic. I know I'm considered damaged in the eyes of the world."

He stared at me, blue eyes piercing my heart, but I couldn't look away. Conflicting emotions crossed his face so quickly I couldn't even identify them, only that he must be warring with himself. After a long minute, he reached up and brushed my cheek with the back of his fingers. When he finally found his voice, it was patient and gentle.

"Georgiana Darcy, you are not damaged—not to God, not to your family, and certainly not to me." His voice rose in volume and exuded a quiet, unshakable vehemence. "And *damn* the rest of the world! You are a precious soul, a remarkable woman—strong and kind and wise." He looked at each feature on my face while he gently touched them in turn—my hair, my brow, my cheek, ending at my mouth. His forefinger ran across my bottom lip, and I shivered. "You are...lovely." An undercurrent of quiet peace diffused across his features. Suddenly, it seemed his internal struggle was over.

"You deserve better, but God help me, I do love you so." He softly kissed my mouth, my damp cheeks, my temple, my forehead. I choked out a little sob, and he swallowed it with another kiss—more urgent this time—and clasped me to him. My arms wound around his neck, fingering the wet locks of his hair, and I opened my mouth under his.

He pulled back to look at me in wonder. I hugged him tightly, resting my chin on his shoulder and closing my eyes.

"I've loved you for"—I laughed through my tears—"well, it seems like forever. You make me happy, and when you are with me, I am fearless."

"Mama?" A little voice piped up from the doorway. Maggie stood there, rubbing her eyes and blinking in the light.

"Oh!" I stepped back hurriedly from Richard and turned around to wipe my eyes. "What is it, darling? Are you all right?"

"I'm thirsty."

"Here." I reached for a glass from the cupboard and filled it from the tap, thankful for the few extra seconds that gave me to compose myself.

Richard sat down at the table in a daze. Maggie climbed up in the chair across from him and swung her legs back and forth while she took a drink, eyeing him carefully.

"Where's your shirt?" she asked.

"Ah…" He looked down, as if he was surprised it was gone.

I broke in hastily. "It was wet, darling. Sheriff took it off to dry it before he went home."

"Oh. Boys can do that, but girls can't."

"That's right. Are you finished with your drink now?"

Maggie nodded, keeping her eyes fixed on Richard. She raised an eyebrow.

"Let's tuck you back in then."

She slid off the chair and shuffled to the door. "G'night, Sheriff."

"'Night, sugar bean."

She pursed her lips in a little frown but said nothing as she followed me back to her room.

I returned after a couple of minutes, smiling apologetically.

"What did the little imp say?"

"Nothing—which means something will come out at an inopportune moment, I'm sure."

Richard grinned. Slowly, however, his expression turned sober. He reached for my hand and guided me toward the chair. I sat down, my eyes never leaving his.

"So, what do we do now?" he asked me.

"Must we do something?" I asked him, feeling distracted and dreamy.

"Perhaps not this minute, but I hope your ending of this little revelation matches mine. It involves a church, a preacher, and your brother's blessing. Although, maybe not in that order, now that I think on it."

That brought me right back to earth.

"Second thoughts, honey?" His voice broke, and he cleared his throat.

I looked up at him quickly. "Oh no! Not at all. I—I don't want to hurry this. I—"

"I don't like keeping secrets, Georgiana. Especially from William."

"William. I hadn't thought that far ahead." I put my hand to my forehead, rubbing it while I closed my eyes.

"You think he'll have a problem with this? With us?"

"Yes. No. I don't know, maybe. There have been so many changes so fast. He got married only recently, and then I moved out only a couple of weeks ago. Can we just…take our time with this?"

"What do you mean?"

"I don't want to rush. I've lived as a married woman, but I've never been courted—not really. I want to enjoy falling in love for the last time in my life, without anyone else intruding, at least for a little while. Would you be willing to do that?"

"Willing to court you?" Richard grinned and replied in a deep, lazy drawl. "Miss Darcy, I'm lookin' forward to it."

Liquid fire surged through my entire body. Somehow, I managed to answer him. "So, we'll tell William, I promise. Just not yet."

A wicked blue light shone from his eyes. "He's a newlywed. He's got no time to worry 'bout us."

"Exactly right." I smiled brightly.

"By end of summer, though, he needs to know. Agreed?"

"Agreed."

"I should be getting back."

"Must you go?" I could hear the wistful tone in my voice.

"Yes, I must. All this stirred up feelings inside me that are particularly powerful from lack of use. I need to go home now, before... Well, I just need to go." He stood up and went to retrieve his shirt and came back in the kitchen, putting his arms in the sleeves as he walked. He shivered when the cold, damp cloth touched his back and shoulders. "But I'll be back to see you soon, darling girl." He buttoned up and reached for me. He pulled me to him, planting a noisy kiss on my lips.

"Richard!" I exclaimed, my cheeks turning pink even though no one was there to see us.

"Good night." He laid his cheek against my temple.

"Good night," I whispered back.

And without another word, he dashed out into the rainy dark.

I hugged myself tightly. I felt like singing, like laughing, like dancing. I bit my lip and grinned, giving a little twirl around the front room before I sank down on the couch in blissful oblivion.

CHAPTER 11

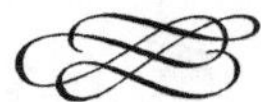

A knock sounded at the screen door. I stood, lifted Ruth to my hip, and headed toward the front of the cottage. Richard's profile was staring off into the distance, but he turned at the sound of my footsteps and sent me one of his easy-going smiles. My heart fluttered in my chest, and I tried to hide my absurdly huge grin as I lifted the hook on the door and pushed it open.

"Hello, darling girl." He kissed my cheek as he stepped through the doorway and tousled Ruth's blond curls. "Hi there, cutie pie."

Ruth reached for him and uttered something unintelligible that Maggie insisted was "Sheriff."

"Make a fella something cool to drink?" he asked, giving me a pointed look. He nodded his head toward the kitchen.

"Be glad to." I turned to Maggie. "Darling, would you play babies with Ruth for a little bit while I make some iced tea for the sheriff?"

"Yes, Mama. Come on, Ruthie." Richard set the little one down, and Maggie took Ruth's hand to lead her away.

I walked to the sink and filled the kettle. Richard came up behind me, sliding his arms around my waist. He drew me against him and deeply inhaled the lavender scent he'd said he loved.

"Richard, if you don't let me go, I can't put the kettle on."

He chuckled and loosened his grip. I stepped over and struck a kitchen match to light the stove. "You're out here early."

"Came out to see William."

"Oh?"

"And you." He grinned mischievously.

"Oh. Good."

"Only Will's out in the field somewhere or so Mrs. Darcy said. I left a message with her."

"Did you have something in particular to tell me? You seemed pretty keen on getting me alone in here." I walked into his arms. "Or was that just a ploy so we could do this." I pulled his head down and kissed him.

Richard pulled my hands from around his neck and held them as he led me to a chair.

"What's wrong?" I asked, leaning over to stroke his cheek. He turned to my palm and kissed it, looking pleased at my response to his lips against my skin. He took my hands in his once more.

"I got word from Brighton, 'bout a man looking for work over there."

"Oh?"

"A man by the name of George Wilson. From the description I gave, the police chief over there thinks he could be George Wickham, but they got no proof. The varmint is slippery as an eel, and we can't seem to catch him."

"Is that why you came to see William?"

"Yes. He needs to be on the lookout, I think."

"Were you planning to tell me at all? Or just leave me out here in blissful ignorance?" A defiant streak mushroomed inside me, and my voice hardened like steel. "I have children, Richard. I need to protect them from that man. I can't do that if you hide information from me."

He looked surprised at my reaction. "You have a point, and that's why I came out here. You do need to know but so does William. I wish—"

"What?"

"If we were married already, I could keep you with me. There would be no worries about your safety or the little ones'. You'd definitely be out of harm's way, no matter where the fiend was."

My face softened. "I'm safe here, Richard. This is my home. My brother is just up the road. George wouldn't dare show his face here, or in Meryton, for that matter. There's a warrant for his arrest, and William and I can both identify him."

Richard shook his head. "I don't know. I don't like it, that's for sure. He's never come this close to you since William chased him off. If it's truly him, that is."

"That's right," I reminded him. "It may not even be my George."

Richard looked up at me sharply. "Don't ever call him your George," he said vehemently. "Not ever."

"Of course not."

"He never deserved you."

"I meant, the George I knew."

He lifted me from the chair and clasped his arms around me, holding me tight. "I won't let him hurt you, darling girl, or the babies."

"I know you won't." I pulled back and looked into the icy, hard blue of his eyes. "I trust you and William to take care of me, and I will watch out for myself too."

"Too right, you will. No trips alone into town, or anywhere, for that matter. Don't open the door until you identify exactly who it is." He muttered, half to himself. "We need to get a phone installed out here. I'll talk to William about it."

"Is that really necessary?"

"Yes, but it may take a while to get the lines all run. I'll call about it first thing tomorrow."

"I'll be fine." I leaned in to kiss him, and he pulled me to him roughly and lifted me to sit on the kitchen table, devouring my mouth as if he couldn't bear to part from me. He was standing between my knees and pressing my body into his in a suggestive manner. He pulled back, resting his forehead on mine, and I let out a frustrated little moan.

"Oh God, Richard, you feel so good!"

He grunted softly.

"You know, I dream about you almost every night."

He smiled. "Now that's what a man likes to hear. It's good for my pride."

"Don't tease me."

"I'm not teasing." He was trying to cool his ardor with humor, but it was a hopeless cause. "What do you dream, honey?"

"I just dream you: you holding my hand, you kissing me, walking beside me." I looked up at him through lowered lashes. "Holding me in my bed."

He shut his eyes. "Now who's teasing who?" he whispered.

I laughed softly. "I'm sorry."

He took a step back. His eyes held a bewildered look, but he was smiling. "I can't believe all this time I thought you were shy and quiet."

"I am, except when I'm with you."

He brought my hand to his lips. "I love you."

"I love you too. Don't worry. Everything will be all right." I stood up and put my arms around his neck, embracing him.

"I hope you're right. I wish I had your faith, darling girl. But then, I never been where you've been. God seen you through that valley. I suppose He'll see you through this one too."

CHAPTER 12

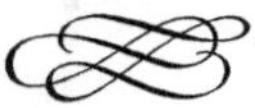

JULY 3, 1933

J scribbled furiously on the yellowed page of my journal. I had neglected writing in it since the spring began, but the confinement necessitated by my former husband's appearance afforded me more free time than I'd had in quite a while.

Something is wrong at the big house. I've taken the girls to see William three times in the last week, and he's never at home. Mrs. Reynolds says he's out in the field, or up at town, and what's more, Elizabeth isn't home either. It's like she's vanished from Pemberley. I haven't even seen her at church. Something is wrong, very wrong. Is she sick? Why would he not tell me? Did they have an argument? Did she, God forbid, leave him? And if so, why? What is going on?

Oh! How I hate not being able to come and go as I please! I despise George Wickham for making us all live in fear like this again! The girls know something is happening, but they're too young to understand what it is. All I do is sit around here and stew about what might be taking place over there in Brighton. Over the last couple days, I've actually begun looking forward to

Deputy Mercer's visit each morning and afternoon. At least, there's some adult to talk to when he's here.

Of course, Richard's been here too—four times in the last week—which has been wonderful. But he's on edge as well. When I asked him if he knew anything about Elizabeth and William, he gruffly informed me that he didn't interfere in married people's trials and tribulations, and he suggested I adopt the same policy.

Even Mrs. Reynolds avoids my eyes when she tells me Elizabeth is visiting her family—again.

I'm so worried...

The rattle of a truck engine made me lift my head from my journal. I looked over at the clock and noticed the time, twelve-thirty. Deputy Mercer was early this afternoon; he didn't usually show up until sometime after one o'clock. Perhaps he had some news. Perhaps George had finally been apprehended, and my life could return to normal.

I swung Ruth up to my hip and approached the door. The curtain obscured his face, but the visitor was Mercer's height.

"Mama!" Maggie yelled as she barreled in from the next room. "Is it Unca? Or Sheriff?"

I looked over my shoulder as I opened the door. "It's Deputy Mercer, darling, you can go—"

I stopped suddenly. Maggie had frozen in place, her eyes round. "Mama?" Her voice was deadly quiet. "Who's that man?"

I whirled around and tried to slam the door shut, but the intruder was too quick, and he strong-armed his way into the house. The stench of old whiskey and stale cigar smoke rolled off him in waves, and there was menace in his bloodshot eyes.

"Hello, my little wife. I've come to fetch you home."

For a moment, I was frozen in fear. *What is he doing here? I can turn him in. William can turn him in. Is he mad?* I calmed myself the way I used to and eyed him carefully. *Mad or not, he's three sheets to the wind.* I cleared my throat and began to speak, bringing my voice under control. If I could just keep him talking until Mercer got here!

"Good afternoon, Mr. Wickham."

"Aww, now Georgie—none of this Mr. Wickham business. I've come home to you, doll. I've missed you." He turned his bleary gaze on the little girl frozen in the middle of the room and held his arms out. "How you doing, Meggie? Come see Daddy, sweetheart."

"No!" Maggie ran to me and clutched my skirt, hiding behind me and not looking at him. She began to cry.

Wickham stood up straight and lowered his arms. "I guess she doesn't remember me."

My guess is that she does. "I think you need to leave now. You're scaring my daughter, and you're not welcome here."

"So, Darcy finally poisoned your mind against me, didn't he? 'Course, I expected as much. I'll never be good enough for the Princess of Pemberley."

"Please leave." I tried to keep my voice quiet, yet commanding.

"I came here to try and talk some sense into you. I know we can be happy, like we used to, remember? We had some good times at the beginning." He sniffed and looked at me with watery eyes.

"I'm not going with you. My life is here now."

"No!" Wickham yelled and swiped at the lamp on the end table next to the sofa. It crashed to the floor and broke into several pieces, making me jump almost out of my skin. Ruth began to wail in fear at the noise.

"What's wrong with that one?" George indicated the crying toddler. "Is she slow or something?"

"She's afraid of loud noises."

"Oh, yeah. Well, sorry about that. It was an accident," he mumbled.

"George"—I tried to reason with him—"you're on the lam. You don't want a woman and children slowing you down." I eased Ruth down and tried to pull her around behind me, but she clung to my leg, crying. I went on, trying to lull him into complacency with my voice. "You want to be free, right? We'd just fence you in. I promise you're better off without us."

His eyes clouded over, and he choked up a little. "My Georgie. You always were so unselfish, so pure and sweet. I loved that about you.

You're not like those other sluts, scheming and plotting and whoring around. It's not too late for us. We can make it work, baby. I know I messed up."

I said nothing.

"Damn it!" he yelled suddenly. "Just come with me. We'll make a new start somewhere." He tried to lower his voice. "It'll be different this time, I promise. We'll have your money to live on."

"Get out of here, George, now!"

The next quarter hour inched by as I watched the man I had once thought so handsome pace back and forth, sit down, stand up, and begin pacing again. He looked haggard and older than his years. Fast living was catching up to him quickly.

He told me of his travels from town to town, how no one would give him a chance, how he wanted to settle down, how he missed me and "Meggie." I gave out several platitudes to try and calm him, alternating them with requests to leave. This went on for endless, angst-filled minutes until he mentioned my trust fund again. *So, that's why he's here now. Where did he learn about that?* I had never told him about my money—initially because he seemed to love me without it, and then later because I would never let him get a hold of it. Suddenly, in a scene from my worst nightmare, he snatched Ruth up from in front of me. The baby screamed in terror, and at that point, I lost all sense. I thought I might faint, but instead I heard myself pleading.

"No! Please! Give her to me, please! Please, George! I'll give you anything you want."

Then I heard a filthy name come out his mouth and felt the sting of his knuckles on my cheek, and suddenly chaos ensued right before my eyes. Perhaps I was hallucinating. I saw Richard sliding silently into the room, pistol trained on George and telling him to give me Ruth back. Then she was in my arms. I automatically whispered words of maternal comfort, not knowing what I said. Numbly, I watched as William slowly lowered his rifle a couple of minutes later. Richard jerked on Wickham's handcuffed arm, and Mercer led him roughly away. I realized that my sister-in-law was embracing me tightly. She then sat down on the couch, holding and comforting the children. *When did Elizabeth arrive?*

I stood immobile, staring at Richard. There was a look of hard triumph in his eyes, and then I saw his gaze sweep to my cheek. An anguished expression crossed his face. He would blame himself for that bruise, because he had promised to protect me. Strangely enough, I now felt completely safe for the first time in years. Richard came to me in my hour of need. I rushed into his arms and began to weep, his name bubbling up from the depths of my soul. I lifted my head off his shoulder and focused on the firm lines of his mouth as they moved in words of reassurance that I couldn't even process. And then, in front of my brother and sister-in-law, my daughters and his co-workers, I kissed him full on the mouth.

CHAPTER 13

JULY 5, 1933

 We approached the big house, all four of us hand in hand, not speaking a word. By some stroke of luck, or cruel quirk of fate, William happened to be sitting alone on the front porch, watching our approach with that awful scowl of his. I'd forgotten how unnerving that stare was when it was turned on me.

We ascended the steps slowly, and Richard squeezed my hand and nodded toward the door.

I hesitated for a second before deciding that all this cold silence was ridiculous. I was a grown woman, after all. "Good morning, William," I said, my head held high.

"Morning, Gi," he answered, but his eyes remained on Richard.

Richard leaned over and whispered in my ear. "Go on inside, darling girl. We'll be along in a minute."

I walked to the door and pulled it open. The girls ran into the kitchen, calling for Mrs. Reynolds and cookies and milk. When I turned to look at the men one last time, they were eyeing each other warily, like two cocks in a barnyard. I rolled my eyes and went in the house. *Men!* I walked through the foyer, around to the parlor window. What luck! It was open, giving me a perfect view of them. The screen would conceal my presence, if I didn't stand too close.

Richard walked over and stood in front of the swing, hands in his pockets, and rearranged his face into his easy-going smile. William remained sitting with his back to the window, stopping the swing's movement abruptly with his foot.

"'Morning, Darcy."

"Fitzwilliam. I was wondering when I might hear from you."

"Yep, I got something to tell you, but I'm pretty sure you've already figured that out."

My brother sighed heavily, as if the weight of the world was on his shoulders.

"I want to marry her, William. I'm asking for your blessing."

"I guess I should be grateful you want to marry her, after that public display of affection in front of the girls, my wife, and your gossiping deputies. Everyone in the county will know about this by now."

Richard gave him a sheepish grin. His cheeks got a little red, but he refused to let my brother, who was eight years his junior, intimidate him. "Those were extraordinary circumstances, you have to admit. Maybe you need to give her a little leeway."

William shrugged. "Maybe." He cleared his throat. "How long has this clandestine little courtship been going on?"

Richard drew his mouth into a thin line and narrowed his eyes at his longtime friend. The two of them stared each other down for several seconds until Richard finally grinned and shook his head. He leaned back lazily against the porch rail, one hand on each side of him. "Nope. Don't think I'll kowtow to the Darcy stare and submit to an interrogation. But I will tell you what you need to know: I love her, she loves me, and we're getting married. We want your approval, but we'll tie the knot without it, if we have to. Now, are you with us or against us?"

"Have you thought at all about the difference in your ages,

Richard? You could almost be her father. What happens when you're seventy and she's fifty-five?"

"We have discussed it. She said we'll cross that bridge when we come to it, but it's a small price to pay for being married to the love of your life."

William slowly shook his head. "Hmmph." He paused for several seconds, lost in his own thoughts, and Richard didn't interrupt him. Finally, William spoke again. "You know, I almost feel a little sorry for you. Don't let her shy, quiet demeanor fool you. My sister has a will of iron, and it's been my experience that she usually gets what she wants."

I was floored and a little indignant at my brother's remark. *Isn't that the pot calling the kettle black?*

Richard laughed good-naturedly. "Yes, I'm finding that out." His face quieted into a smile. "Good thing I'd do most anything for her then, isn't it?" He continued. "It's easy to forgive that stubborn streak in people, when what they want is generally for the good of those they love."

William nodded after a minute, and I realized he knew that Richard was speaking, not only of me, but of him as well. I marveled anew at Richard's uncanny ability to convey two or three messages with just a few words. I hoped my brother received this one loud and clear. Any interference on William's part would not be tolerated, but his attempts might be forgiven, because we knew how much he cared about us.

Apparently, William had one more issue to resolve, however.

"What about my nieces?"

"What about them? They'll be my family. I'll take care of them."

"Even though they're not yours?"

Richard looked offended. "They are mine, far as I'm concerned. The way I see it, I've been given a mighty privilege, the chance to raise a family after all."

William stood and ambled over to stand beside Richard, leaning back against the porch rail in the same posture. He shrugged again. "You're lucky. I'm in a generous and forgiving mood."

"I am lucky, and that's for certain."

"Elizabeth knew something was happening between the two of you. She tried to tell me back in the spring."

Richard raised his eyebrows. "It seems Mrs. Darcy is quite observant. We hardly knew it ourselves at that point in time. What did you tell her?"

William smirked. "I said it was impossible."

"Nothing is impossible."

"No."

"Mrs. Darcy doin' all right after our ordeal with Wickham the other day?"

William's dimpled smile spread across his face. "Yes, she is doing very well."

"Georgiana was worried about the two of you a few days ago."

His face clouded. "We had a rough patch there, but everything's fine now."

"Good."

There was a long pause before William went on. "You have my blessing, old friend. Do take care of them though. They are very precious to me."

Richard put out his hand. "I will. You have my word on that, William, my solemn vow."

William stood up straight and shook the offered hand. "You mentioned Wickham just now—is the scoundrel taken care of?"

"He's in federal custody, awaiting trial, with no bond because he's considered a flight risk. With all the charges they got racked up against him, plus the ones he's just incurred here, I think he'll go to jail for a very long time."

"That is well then."

"Yes."

"Is my sister listening from the parlor window?"

I took a step back, startled. *Darn you, William!* He knew me too well for comfort.

William chuckled. "I'll bet she is." He paused. "Gigi?"

I was already at the front door, pushing it open. "Is it safe to come out?"

My brother held his arms open. His eyes were suspiciously shiny. "Congratulations, Gi."

I ran to hug him. "Thank you!" I turned to Richard and threw my arms around him as well. "You were right. I was fretting for nothing, no reason at all!"

* * *

A FEW DAYS LATER, Richard sat in the parlor of my cottage, looking into a pair of dark brown eyes that absorbed every detail of his expression. Maggie stood before him, watching as he explained that in a few months he would marry her mother and join her family.

"So, when you marry Mama, you'll be my godfather."

"Umm… not exactly. I'll be your step-father."

She shook her head. "No."

Richard looked up at me, bewildered; he hadn't anticipated Maggie refusing her "consent," but I knew my daughter well enough to ask for an explanation.

"Tell me why Sheriff will be your godfather, darling."

Maggie looked at me in exasperation, as if the answer were obvious. Then she turned to Richard and explained patiently. "You're gonna be my godfather because God gave you to me."

Richard swallowed hard. I felt my own throat close up with emotion. My amazing, insightful daughter! I was awestruck at the profound wisdom in her reasoning.

"Well, that makes sense, I suppose, although other people may still call me your step-father. But you and Mama and I, we'll know different, won't we?"

Maggie nodded and turned as if to go, but then she stopped and looked back at Richard. "That man who used to be my father, the one that came here and made Mama cry and hit her."

Richard winced at the blunt force of those words.

She continued. "He's gone, isn't he?"

"Yes, he's gone—far away, and the law will keep him away from you and Ruth and your mama forever."

She looked thoughtful. "He was…" She fished for a word that didn't come, waving her hand in mild frustration. "Wrong. He was wrong. Father was the wrong job for him. So, God fired him and gave you the job instead. I heard you say it that day."

"Say what?"

"He didn't deserve a sweet child. He did a bad job."

Richard looked up at me again.

I smiled at him. "Watch what you say, Richard. She doesn't miss a thing."

He touched Maggie's cheek. "No, sugar bean, he didn't deserve you, any of you, and I wanted the job, so when your mama offered it to me, I gladly took it."

"That is well then." She nodded seriously, in an uncanny imitation of her Unca.

CHAPTER 14

SEPTEMBER 5, 1933

"You never talk about Evelyn."

Richard looked down at the piece of clover in his fingers, twirling it in an absent-minded manner. He and I had slipped away for a couple of hours while William and Elizabeth had the girls one afternoon.

Cautiously, he responded to my understated query. "I wasn't sure if that was something you wanted to hear. What good would come of it?"

"It's just…You know everything about George—how it all began, how bad it was, how it ended. I know nothing about your first wife at all. I barely remember her."

"I didn't know you ever met her," he replied, surprised.

"Maybe once or twice. I think she might have been at my father's funeral with you."

"Ah."

"I thought she was pretty."

"I thought so too."

"Were you happy with her?"

"Yes, I believe so. We weren't married for very long, before she passed."

I spun around from my perch beside him and laid my head against his thigh, picking up several of the clover stems beside me and looping them together to make a chain. After a few minutes, I spoke, my voice trembling ever so slightly.

"It's hard to live up to a ghost."

"Is that what you think you have to do?"

I shrugged. "She was good to you. It's not like with George and me. You know I'll never wish you were him. But you and Evelyn loved each other. Maybe…"

I wanted his reassurance, but I wasn't sure how to ask for it. He reached down and stroked my hair.

"Darling girl, how can I explain it to you?" He looked off into the distance for a long minute. Had I upset him or made him angry? Suddenly, he looked back down at me. "You see that tree over there?" He pointed.

"The crooked one with the big knot in it?"

He nodded. "The very one. Now, I happen to know for a fact that several years ago, that tree was struck by lightning."

"Really?"

"Saw it myself. I was out here hunting when it happened and trying to get back home. When the tree was struck, a huge branch came tumbling off and landed on the ground.

"Where the branch was severed, there was a gaping wound in the bark of the tree—jagged, sharp edges all around it, very ugly. I didn't think the tree would survive that injury. But, over the next few years the rain flooded the hole, and the sun warmed it, and the wind softened the sharp edges and made that little hollow that you see now. The hole is still there, and it changed the way the tree grew, but it's still a good tree—maybe even stronger than it would have been otherwise. I'll never know for sure."

"And Evelyn's and the baby's deaths are the lightning storm, and you are the tree, and you have a hole in your heart like the hollow in the tree?"

"I see you catch my meaning, and you're right, but there's more to the story. Let me tell you what I found in that tree last spring."

I looked up at him, waiting.

"A robin made her nest in it, and that old damaged tree sheltered that robin." He ran his finger down my nose and leaned over to kiss my mouth. "And her little chicks."

I laughed. "So, in that scenario, I guess I'm the robin, and Maggie and Ruth are the little chicks." I turned and looked at the tree. "Although, I think I'd rather be a bluebird than a robin."

It was his turn to laugh, a little chuckle that made my stomach bubble up and warmth spread to my toes. I curled them inside my shoes.

His expression turned serious. "I did love Evelyn and the baby, and you can still see the scar when you look for it. Yet I recovered, and I managed to survive and accept. I promise you, there is enough love in me for you and the young'uns to last a lifetime. 'The more I give to thee, the more I have, for both are infinite.'"

I recognized the quote and smiled. "Shakespeare?" Then, I frowned. "*Romeo and Juliet?*"

He laughed.

I sat up and leaned in to kiss him. "I love the way you explain things, almost like a parable."

"I figure if it worked for Jesus, it should work for a humble farm boy like me. I'll just try to follow His example." His arms closed around me, and I wriggled into his lap.

I stroked his cheek with my hand and laid my head against his shoulder. "You must have been so lonely after their passing. George broke my heart, but at least I had Maggie and Ruth to keep me busy."

"Yes," he said simply.

"Was there no one to comfort you?" I stopped, suddenly aware of what I'd asked. "I'm sorry, that's not any of my business." I tried to sit up and look away, but he brought my chin back around to face him.

"I had no lady friend, if that's what you mean." His blue eyes held mine, a knowing kindness in his gaze. "Every once in a while, I might take a woman to the picture show, or a dance, but there was no one to *comfort* me, as you say. A man in my job, well, it wouldn't do to be… loose with women. Not that it would be right in any case, but especially not in mine."

I found words tumbling out of my mouth, unbidden. That was another thing that amazed me about Richard, his ability to draw out my innermost thoughts with just the compassion in his eyes. "I'm glad there wasn't anyone else. I'm selfish enough to be happy about it, even though I know you were lonely. It's unkind of me."

He shook his head. "You're not unkind. I think that's just human nature. I'm glad you care enough to want me for yourself, because I feel the same about you."

"I do want you," I said in earnest. "I love you, and I want to make you happy." I eased off his lap and hiked my skirt up around my hips. I straddled him and leaned in to his embrace.

"Gi?" he choked out.

I lovingly stroked his hair, his face, his brow, chin, shoulders, chest —to memorize this moment, sear into my brain what he looked like. "From the minute I see you walk into a room, I want to be this close to you." I kissed him long and deep. "You just draw me in. Let me show you how much I adore you." I reached for his shirt buttons and began to undo them. He grabbed my hands, gritting his teeth as he stopped me.

"Gi, please…"

"Yes," I whispered softly, almost mindless with want. "Please. I want to please you. Let me."

Suddenly, his body roared to life, pushing me backwards until I was on my back with my legs wrapped around him. He devoured me with kisses, rocking against me in an almost forgotten rhythm.

He pulled back, his honor and his desire warring in his expression. It made me want him all the more.

"We aren't bound yet."

"What?"

"I'm not promised to you yet."

"So…promise."

"What?" He pulled back farther, confused.

"Promise. Here. Now."

"This isn't funny, Georgiana." He rolled off me and to the side.

I followed, turning on my side and facing him. "I don't need a dress and a ceremony to know you'll keep your promise. I know the man you are." I kissed him. "My best friend." I kissed his jaw. "My protector." I ran my hand down his back and around to his belt, drawing an involuntary moan from his chest. "My lover," I whispered in his ear, bringing my other hand up to unbuckle his belt and open his trousers. "Promise me."

"Hell, I'll promise you anything you want."

I smiled. "Then, repeat after me. I, Richard…" I slid my hand up and stroked his face.

"I, Richard…" He rolled back half on top of me.

"Take you, Georgiana…" I pushed his trousers over his hips. He repeated after me, moving over and reaching between us to remove my panties. He got them to my knees before I reached up with one foot and pushed them the rest of the way off.

"To be my wife." He went on. "From this day forward. For better or worse…" He kissed my cheek softly and ran his hand up and down my arm. "For richer or poorer. In sickness and in health." He ran a finger from my hairline to the delicate edge of my chin. "To love and to cherish…" His voice became softer, his expression serious. "Till death do us part." He blinked his eyes rapidly, forcing the tears away. "And thereto I pledge thee my faith," he finished simply.

My breath hitched in my throat. What had begun as a gentle tease had turned into a heartfelt declaration of his love for me that moved my very soul. I stared at him and let out a shaky sigh. "Richard Fitzwilliam, I will love you for the rest of my life."

He moved back over me and held himself above me, waiting. "For me, this means forever. After this, there's no turning back, honey."

I nodded, and my eyes shut in bliss. Finally, I was where I needed to be. This was right. This was home.

CHAPTER 15

OCTOBER 8, 1933

*R*ichard knocked at the door of the cottage, but I couldn't rouse myself to answer. We were usually all up at the crack of dawn, and it was now eight thirty. He used his key and let himself in, and Maggie went down the hallway to greet him.

"Hi, Sheriff," she said cheerfully.

"Hello, Maggie, how are you this morning?"

"I'm fine."

"That's good."

"Mama's sick."

His voice changed instantly. "She's sick? What's the matter?"

"She's in the bathroom 'losing her breakfast.' That's what she called it. How do you lose something that's inside your belly? And her breakfast isn't lost, because I know exactly where it is now."

Richard hurried down the hall to the bathroom. The door was open, and I was sitting on the tub, resting my head on my arms. I looked up and offered him a weak smile. "'Morning."

"Darling girl, are you all right?"

I nodded. "Let's go out on the porch. I think I need some air."

He helped me up and led me to the door. Maggie and Ruth followed, clutching their baby dolls and a pinwheel he'd brought them back from town the other day. Maggie busied herself with the pinwheel out in the yard, while Ruth put her head and upper body through the tire swing, gliding back and forth on her tummy. Richard led me to the glider and sat down next to me, drawing my hand into his.

"Do you need the doctor?" he asked, worried.

"No, I'll be fine in an hour or two. It doesn't last much longer than that."

"How long has this been going on?" He stopped and stared at me in sudden realization. "Georgiana? You're pregnant?"

I looked down and nodded. "I'm pretty sure. I've been through this twice before."

He whistled and sat back in the glider. "Well now, this is unexpected. I mean, it's not like I didn't know it was a possibility, but—"

"I'm sorry if you're upset"—I went on in a quiet voice—"but I'm not. I can't bring myself to regret loving you, and I'll never regret that I'm going to have your child."

He took my hand again. "I'm not upset, honey. A little scared maybe. You know why."

I brought my other hand up to caress his jaw. "Don't be scared. The doctor who delivered Ruth said I was made for having babies."

"Babies," he muttered to himself. "My, my, my." He drew my head to his shoulder and kissed it. We sat in silence, the creak of the glider the only sound besides the occasional little girl voice and the chirp of a bird. The wind stirred around us, gently enveloping us in the scent of crisp morning air and falling leaves.

"Feeling better?"

I nodded. The glider rocked back and forth, back and forth, and gradually, came to stop.

"You wanna go get married today?"

I sat up. "What?"

"I'll marry you today. I'd be happy to. Make all this official, instead of just between us."

I threw my arms around him. "Goodness, you're sweet! It's no wonder I love you so." I laid my head back on his shoulder, but not before I caught the embarrassed smile and flushed cheeks. "The wedding's in two weeks. My brother spent a mint on my dress and the reception. I say we just go ahead with what we've planned. In the greater scheme of things, a few days won't matter either way."

He sighed. "I suppose you're right."

We sat quietly for several more minutes, absorbing the fall sunshine. Richard chuckled deep in his chest. I smiled happily.

"What is it?"

"I think the world just turned upside down and tilted sideways. Everything looks different, brighter somehow."

"Yes," I replied softly. "Isn't it wonderful?"

CHAPTER 16

I watched as Richard handed our baby daughter over to her Uncle William. William's eyes shone as he smiled down into the little face with the bright blue eyes. She was such a sweet baby —slept well, ate well, rarely cried. She already had her daddy's smile.

I leaned over the table and picked up a roll to put on Ruth's plate. Mrs. Reynolds was supervising Maggie with hers. Maggie had developed an independent streak and insisted she could fix her own plate now. It was probably a good thing, though, as I was busier than ever with three little girls under the age of seven.

Today was a celebration at Pemberley. A big luncheon was being given in honor of our baby girl's christening, an event that took place earlier that morning at Harvey's Ridge Methodist church. Mrs. Reynolds was in her element, directing the girls she hired to cater the affair. Mrs. Darcy, she insisted, was unable to help because she had given birth only five months ago.

Joseph Darcy was sitting on his mother's lap, giggling at Ruth as she made silly faces at him. It was obvious to everyone that Joseph had his mother's friendly and outgoing disposition. He smiled and cooed at everyone who looked at him, and charmed every woman in sight.

The quiet dinners for adults at Pemberley were a thing of the past. Instead of having guests sit and be served during birthdays and other celebrations, Mrs. Reynolds and Elizabeth had resorted to setting up a long buffet table and letting people go through and serve themselves before retreating to the dining room table. Of course, with all the Darcys, Fitzwilliams, Bingleys and Bennets in the mix, we filled the long kitchen table as well. After the children's plates were fixed, but before everyone else began, William called us all together to say grace. Richard leaned over and whispered something in his ear, and William nodded, gesturing for Richard to speak. I was surprised at my husband; he wasn't usually much of a speechmaker. He cleared his throat a little nervously, and then he began:

"I've asked William to let me say the blessing today, but before I do, I just want to thank you all for coming to our little sweetheart's christening. I was looking around the church this morning and seeing all the friendly faces reminded me of how fortunate we are, in this day and time, to have this land, this country and this community. Times have been hard, but we have each other, and I know things will get better, easier for us all as time goes by. I myself, have never felt richer or more blessed, because I have my beautiful wife and my precious little chicks around me."

"Wait till you have five of them." Dr. Bennet's dry voice carried above the crowd. Elizabeth Bennet Darcy rolled her eyes, and everyone else chuckled.

"So," Richard went on, "I'm glad you're all here to welcome our little one, whose name expresses my thoughts on this occasion better than any speech." He took the baby from her uncle and gazed down into her face. "Welcome to your family, little Joy."

Applause and cheers, and cries of "hear, hear!" sounded throughout the room. I looked at Richard through eyes blurred with tears and put my fingers to my lips to blow him a kiss. He beamed at me and then called out, "Please bow your heads and let us give thanks."

I barely listened to the deep cadence of the blessing. Somewhere in the middle of it though, I heard the voice in my soul, the one that directed me back home over three years ago. Again, the words without form appeared in my mind.

"Georgiana, listen." I held my breath and was very still so I could hear.

"You're free."

The End

AUTHOR'S NOTE

The Journey Home is a "side-quel", a companion piece to my award-winning debut novel, *1932*. This novella stands alone, but readers may have fun corresponding the events in this story to that one.

I'd like to shout out to several people who read *The Journey Home* and gave their input—and contributed a suggestion or two—or ten! Thanks are due to Karen Adams, Laura, Betty Jo Moss, and Jane Vivash. Special thanks go to my editor, Christina Boyd, for her expertise and encouragement. I'd also like to thank Cloud Cat Design for creating the beautiful, romantic cover for this book.

If you enjoyed *The Journey Home*, a review on your favorite online bookstore or review website is always welcome, even if it is just a line or two, as it helps other readers know if they might like the story as well. And, if you would like bits of authorly goodness in your inbox each month (updates, sales, book recommendations, etc.) I invite you to receive <u>News & Muse Letter</u> (distributed by MailChimp, addresses are kept confidential). I love to hear from readers, so don't be shy.

Happy Reading!

ALSO BY KAREN M COX

1932

Find Wonder in All Things

Undeceived

I Could Write a Book

Son of a Preacher Man

Anthologies

Sun-Kissed: Effusions of Summer

The Darcy Monologues

Dangerous to Know: Jane Austen's Rakes & Gentlemen Rogues

Rational Creatures (Coming October 2018)